"Brad, this is incredible," Carly sighed.

Forgetting where she was, she turned in her seat to look at him.

"Don't!" he warned sharply.

But he was too late. Carly felt the canoe tilt alarmingly from the shift in her weight, tried to correct, couldn't, and fell flat on her back into the river as they capsized. She heard Brad curse as she went under, and surfaced to hear him still swearing fluently.

"Now Brad," Carly tried to soothe him. But when he pulled her to him, she knew she didn't have any fight left. She met his kiss, lips hot, mobile, eager. Her tongue dueled with his. Her chest burned, and she felt as if her heart had climbed into her throat.

Tearing herself free, she saw the hunger in his dark eyes. She couldn't hide her own desperate yearning, nor did she want to . . .

Dear Reader:

Summer is here! And we've got six new SECOND CHANCE AT LOVE romances to add to your pleasure in the new season. So sit back, put your feet up, and enjoy . . .

You've also got a lot to look forward to in the months ahead—delightful romances from exciting new writers, as well as fabulous stories from your tried-and-true favorites. You know you can rely on SECOND CHANCE AT LOVE to provide the kind of satisfying romantic entertainment you expect.

We continue to receive and enjoy your letters—so please keep them coming! Remember: Your thoughts and feelings about SECOND CHANCE AT LOVE books are what enable us to publish the kind of romances you not only enjoy reading once, but also keep in a special place and read again and again.

Warm wishes for a beautiful summer,

Ellen Edwards

Ellen Edwards
SECOND CHANCE AT LOVE
The Berkley Publishing Group
200 Madison Avenue
New York, N.Y. 10016

Second Chance at Love®

COUNTRY
PLEASURES

LAUREN FOX

**SECOND CHANCE AT LOVE
BOOK**

For Russ Hawkins
(who has finished the Seventy five times)

Other Second Chance at Love books by
Lauren Fox

SPARRING PARTNERS   #177

COUNTRY PLEASURES

First edition published June 1984

First printing

"Second Chance at Love" and the butterfly emblem are trademarks
belonging to Jove Publications, Inc.

Printed in the United States of America

Second Chance at Love books are published by
The Berkley Publishing Group
200 Madison Avenue, New York, NY 10016

Chapter One

"BLOODSUCKER!"

Carly Meadows whirled at the sound of the bellow, wincing as pain shot through her twisted ankle. Muttering curses at herself for ever having gotten involved in such a wild goose chase, she wondered why she had worn open-toed heels for a trip to the boonies.

"Leech!" the powerfully masculine voice added even more forcefully. Carly backed away from the inside door warily. The old-fashioned thumb latch rattled at the same instant there was a loud thud against the wall. It was followed by the sound of something scattering and rattling.

The door was yanked open and a stocky, billiard-ball bald man bulled his way through, head down. As he fumbled desperately with the outside door, something whistled past Carly and shattered against the doorframe, scattering white fragments around the showroom like buckshot. The door finally yielded and the target of the missile fell out into the hard, bright summer sunlight. Carly's last view of him was as he plunged down the precipitous gravel drive, the tails of his plaid sport jacket flapping comically over his broad backside.

Turning, Carly caught her breath when she saw who, apparently, was the source of the missiles and the bellows of fury. She hadn't known the sight of a man to make her knees go weak since high school. But this—specimen— caused her to reach out to steady herself. He was juggling what looked like a lump of hardened modeling clay in one powerful hand. His biceps flexed excitingly, straining the rolled-up sleeves of his plaid shirt. His torso tapered to a narrow waist and trim hips. The belt through his jeans was wide, tooled leather, while the buckle was heavy brass, utilitarian. His muscular forearms were covered with curly black hair and, insanely, Carly found herself wondering what it would feel like to be in the embrace of those arms, what those hands might feel like on her body.

"Something I can do for you?" the man asked in a rich baritone as he put down the clay and lounged against the doorframe.

Carly found herself the object of his intense dark-eyed gaze and suddenly had a crazy urge to run her fingers through his unruly black hair, to comb the wayward locks back off his forehead. "Oh, um, I'm looking for someone," she stammered uncertainly, cursing herself for being overwhelmed by him—even though he was an incredible hunk.

"In the words of an unforgettable little green movie character, 'Found someone you have, I'd say,'" he responded while he insolently inventoried her.

Desperately, as she endured his scrutiny, Carly tried to gather her resources. After nervously pushing at her thick auburn hair, she tried to tuck her pale green blouse more smoothly into the waist of her dark green skirt. His eyes took in her figure, measuring her curves in a way that made her tingle, and she wished crazily that she were taller than five feet two, so his study would take longer.

"I'm looking for an artist," she explained awkwardly. "I think I have the wrong place." She gestured around the showroom with its selection of cast-iron wood-burning stoves, rustic furniture, rack of strange-looking canoe paddles, and welter of outdoors books and gadgets.

"An artist, is it?" he inquired, easing his weight off the doorframe to move completely into the room. Suddenly the room seemed much smaller than it had.

"I'm trying to find a sculptor by the name of Brad Weston," Carly explained, desperately clinging to the shreds of her composure.

"I'm Brad Weston."

Carly gulped. She felt intimidated by the way she had to look up at him when he got close to her—he was a foot taller than she was, at least. She was relieved when he planted one hip on a stove, because that way he wasn't quite so tall and imposing. "I don't suppose there's another Brad Weston around here?" she managed to comment lightly.

"Not to my knowledge." He seemed infernally pleased with her floundering.

"The man I'm looking for is a sculptor," she elaborated, wondering what she was going to have to do to get herself steadied down. "A wood-carver," she added when his eyes showed no hint of recognition. She wanted to reach out and brace herself with a hand on his arm.

"A whittler?" he suggested, his words summoning up an image of an old man rocking back in his chair, peeling slivers off a stick with a big pocket knife.

"You sell stoves," Carly noted, trying to retrieve the situation somehow.

"Among other things," he acknowledged easily, waving vaguely.

Carly found his laconic answers nettling. "Anything else?" she asked.

"Oh, sure. Canoes, bicycles, cross-country skis. Depends on what's in season."

"What's that smell?" Carly asked, wrinkling her nose at the penetrating chemical aroma. It reminded her of burning plastic, like the time her shower curtain had gotten stuck to the portable heater.

"Oh, that's from my main business," he explained easily. "I build canoes."

"I beg your pardon?"

"I build canoes," he repeated.

"That's what I thought you said."

"Something wrong with that? Someone has to build them."

"Oh, I didn't mean it that way," Carly assured him, wondering why he put her on the defensive all the time. "It's just not the kind of thing I think of people doing in an old barn."

"It's got to be done somewhere," he pointed out reasonably.

"I suppose so," she agreed inanely. Then her curiosity got the better of her. "Could I see?" she asked impulsively.

"You want to see how I build canoes?" he asked, as if no one had ever made such a request.

"I've never seen a canoe built," she explained. "Something wrong with that?"

"Just not the kind of thing I ever regarded as a spectator sport," he responded. "Be my guest." He gestured grandly toward the inner door with a sweep of his arm.

"Thanks," Carly replied, feeling more confident. Nevertheless, she carefully sidled past him and brushed against one of the stoves in an effort to avoid touching him. She

could feel the heat of his body across the small space between them.

Her feet crackled over fragments of clay missile as she
went through the door. Memories from her Iowa childhood
told her that the showroom had once been the milk house
of the old barn. The area she was entering now had housed
the livestock. But instead of the gloomy low-ceilinged area
she expected, it turned out to be surprisingly light and airy,
thanks to huge picture windows on the long south side and
a high ceiling. The open expanse was broken up by columns
and beams of unfinished wood that still showed the touch
of ax and adz. Where the hand-hewn framing met, there
were diagonal braces. Everything was held together with
wooden pegs rather than nails.

The chemical stink was stronger. When Carly wrinkled
her nose, Brad Weston reached over and flicked a switch.
A fan began to purr, and Carly felt a cooling draft through
the open door at her back. She looked dubiously down at
the clay shards around her bare toes.

"Sorry about the mess. But I've found it's a good way
to get rid of intruders."

"Mind telling me what he did to upset you, so I don't
do the same thing?"

"Don't worry about it," he answered unhelpfully. "Any-
how, there's a sample of my work."

Carly didn't look where he was pointing because her
gaze had fastened on an exquisite half-finished wood carving. It stood in a corner not far from a wood-burning stove,
this one hooked up to a chimney.

Carly had the feeling the roughed-out beaver was about
to set its teeth into one of the beams holding up the barn.
Even in its unfinished state, the piece had the same incredible impact as the one she'd seen in the window of a local
hardware store less than half an hour before.

"You are Brad Weston!" she exclaimed unthinkingly.

"No kidding," he responded dryly.

"No, I mean you're Brad Weston the sculptor," she elaborated.

"I'm Brad Weston the canoe builder," he responded.

Carly was vaguely aware of a hint of exasperation in his
voice but was too distracted by her study of his carving for

it to penetrate. "Canoe builder," she snorted derisively, not taking her eyes off the beaver.

"You got some kind of a problem with that?" he asked acidly.

Carly realized how patronizing she must have sounded. "I'm sorry, I didn't mean it as a put-down," she apologized.

"Oh, really?" he responded skeptically.

Carly tried to explain and found herself getting in deeper and deeper.

"Never mind," he growled, turning away from her. "Just because a man works with his hands, everyone thinks he's nothing more than a gorilla."

Carly felt her Irish temper rising swiftly. "Now wait a minute!" she said angrily. "That's not what I meant!"

"Well then, just what did you mean?" he demanded.

"I meant it just seems a shame that someone with your talent at carving should be turning out canoes for a living," she explained. "You do beautiful work. Your carvings would sell well down in the city."

"And just why are you so sure of that? You're an expert on the price of wood carvings, I suppose?" he asked sarcastically.

"My name is Carly Meadows. I'm a partner in The Gallery, in New York City," she announced primly. "We're dealers in Americana, selling primarily to decorators and the like. There's a good market for native American crafts, both antique and modern, down in the city. I'm prepared to offer you an exclusive contract to market your work."

"Forget it," he retorted, picking up a ball of hardened clay.

"What?"

"I said forget it," he repeated, starting to toss the clay from one hand to the other. "I'm not interested."

"What? But..." She wished he'd keep still. The missile made her nervous and she kept wondering if the sleeves of his shirt would burst from the strain as the clay continued to move from hand to hand. "But your sculpture is really good. I'm not saying it could make you rich, but..."

"Who said I want to be rich?" he asked.

"But canoes!" she protested, feeling as if they were speaking two different languages.

"Someone's got to make them," he pointed out in that frustratingly dry way he had.

"Why do you keep talking like . . . like you're a garbage collector or something?" she asked, exasperated.

"Isn't that the way you feel about me?" he asked innocently.

"No, it is not! It's just that I don't see why someone with your talent should be wasting time on canoes, of all things!"

"I don't regard it as wasting time," he responded blandly.

Carly took a deep breath. The man had an absolutely infuriating ability to keep her off balance. "A gift like you have, and you'd rather make canoes," she huffed derisively. "It's preposterous."

"Why is it preposterous?"

"Because it's a waste!"

He let out a grunt of exasperation. "If you're just going to stand here and talk in circles, you can leave. I've got more important things to do."

Carly felt herself coming to a slow boil. "You have got to be the most insufferably stubborn, self-centered, obtuse, bull-headed, stiff-necked knothead it has ever been my misfortune to meet. I am offering you the opportunity of a lifetime . . ."

"Now where have I heard that line before?" he inquired dryly. "I think it was a used car salesman. No, I remember now, it was someone trying to sell me an encyclopedia."

"Dammit! I did not drive four hours from New York City to the middle of absolute Nowheresville to be insulted by some stiff-necked country bumpkin who wouldn't recognize opportunity if it bit him!" Carly exploded. Turning, she started toward the door, aggravated that because of her twisted ankle she couldn't stomp out.

"You leaving?" Brad inquired.

"Yes!"

"Well, close the door on your way out," he called.

Finding his calm dismissal absolutely infuriating, Carly slammed the door behind her, crossed the shop in three brisk strides, and banged the outside door closed as hard as she could. Muttering angrily to herself, she lurched her way down the rough drive to the Rent-a-Wreck she'd hired for the trip. Twice, her heel came down on stones, causing ominous warning pains in her ankle.

Artists! Whether they called themselves that or canoe builders, they were without a doubt the most frustrating breed of animal ever put on God's green earth, she reflected sourly.

Once behind the wheel, she glared up the hill at the barn, then savagely twisted the key in the ignition. The result was a mechanical growl that dwindled to a low moan and then a silence that sent her heart down to her toes. Slapping her hand angrily on the steering wheel of the rented Pinto, she tried again, with the same lack of success. She wished the car were a real pinto, so the kick she felt like giving it might have some effect.

Out of the car again, she lifted the hood. Immediately spotting what was wrong, she decided having two older car-crazy brothers did have its uses. Where there should have been a fan belt there was nothing. Sourly, she stared at the empty pulleys, wondering idly and fruitlessly why she hadn't noticed the alternator light on. She knew the symptoms of a dead battery. Raising her head, she gazed around and contemplated her options.

When she'd described it as Nowheresville, she hadn't been exaggerating. Brad Weston's barn was located a good five miles from the nearest state highway and another three from the nearest village. The beauty of the rolling hills, with their rich, dark green woods and drying brown fields, did nothing to ease her mood. Not another house in sight. In fact, she realized, there was no house in sight at all. The only building she could see was Brad Weston's barn.

She looked unhappily up the slope, furious at her lack of choice in the matter. With a sigh of resignation, she headed up the driveway, desperately trying to think up some way to salvage the situation. She had just about managed to assemble what she felt was a witty opening when her heel came down on one of the rocks in the drive. Twenty feet from the barn, she went down in a heap, her ankle a knot of blazing agony that brought tears to her eyes.

For a few moments, all she could do was lie there and try not to faint. Sucking in a breath, she held her ankle while she waited for the spots in front of her eyes to recede.

How she had managed to let her partner talk her into this she would never know. When she got back to the city, she'd kill him.

As she took off her shoes, she found one bright spot. At least, thanks to a summer tan and the warm weather, she hadn't worn stockings. Hesitantly, she got to her feet and put her weight on her sore ankle. It hurt like the devil, but it held. Hobbling, her shoes dangling from her hand, she made her way to the showroom. Her hand was on the latch when the door was jerked open, throwing her off balance. She found herself in Brad Weston's embrace and suddenly she did know how his arms would feel around her. Her entire body reacted with a rush that simultaneously tightened her arms around him and loosened every other muscle in her.

"Well, excuse me," he said, making no move to let her go.

Carly tried to summon her resistance and pry herself loose, without a great deal of success. Finally, she got her hands between them and pushed against his hard chest, her fingers catching in the curly hairs at the base of his throat. His skin was very hot. She could smell him, a delectable mingling of masculine musk and the chemicals he used in his work. She pushed harder on his chest. Making it very clear it was his choice, not hers, he let her go.

"I've got car trouble," she announced unhappily, forgetting all the gems she'd thought of as she'd hobbled up the drive.

"Kind of spoils a good exit, doesn't it?" he inquired astutely.

"It sure does," she admitted. She had a crazy urge to lean against him and decided it'd be safer a few feet away.

"You're limping," he observed, openly concerned as she moved off.

"No kidding!"

"Come here and sit down," he ordered, slipping an arm around her, supporting her as easily as if she weighed half her hundred and ten pounds. She did yield to her instincts this time and leaned contentedly against him. She told herself it was to save her ankle.

After he eased her down in an unfinished captain's chair—another example of his work?—he took her shoes and studied them critically. "Dumb footwear for the country," he pointed out.

"No dumber than having a driveway full of potholes," she retorted, rubbing her ankle.

"Let me see that," he urged, reaching for her leg.

"It's getting better," she argued, not trying to escape his grasp. His hands were firm and strong and his touch on her bare calf made it tingle. He tenderly probed her aching ankle, then gently flexed her foot.

"I don't think it's broken," he announced as she leaned forward to watch. "Just twisted, is my guess."

She nodded, her voice suddenly having deserted her. He slid his hand up her leg, stroking her smooth calf and sending little shivers of excitement through her. His face was very close to hers, but she didn't back off when he closed the two-inch gap. His lips touched hers, and she braced herself with a hand on his shoulder. Under the urging of his lips and the tickling probe of his tongue, the kiss quickly became extremely intimate, anesthetizing her completely to the pain in her ankle. She did manage to stop his fingers before they crept under the hem of her knee-length skirt.

"You're supposed to kiss where it hurts," she managed to point out somehow when they came up for air. Her heart was fluttering like a trapped bird, and it hurt to breathe, and now the spots before her eyes weren't caused by pain.

"My pleasure," he assured her softly, lifting her foot. The touch of his lips on her bare ankle was unlike anything she'd ever felt before in her twenty-eight years.

"I'm all right!" she snapped, more sharply than she meant to, as she retrieved her foot.

"You sure are," he agreed, grinning broadly as he got lightly to his feet.

Desperately, Carly tried to collect her thoughts, tried to figure out how to regain control of the situation. "I need a fan belt," she explained, "and a jump start. I don't suppose you have a fan belt for a Pinto?" She tried to conceal her glowing cheeks by bending over to put her shoes on again.

"I can give you the jump start," he answered, "but it'll take a phone call to get the fan belt. Believe it or not, the telephone has made its way up here to Nowheresville." He held up the receiver demonstratively.

Carly was still trying to recover her equilibrium after his

high-voltage kiss, and his verbal tweaking kept knocking her off balance. She sat back in the chair and twisted and turned her foot to ease the ache. Her pride kept her from apologizing, though she knew she should.

"That should do it," he noted as he hung up. "A friend of mine's headed this way from town, and he'll drop one by."

"Sorry to be such a bother," Carly apologized finally.

"No trouble," he assured her. She looked up at him as he lounged back against one of the cast-iron stoves. He folded his arms across his muscular chest, again threatening the seams of his shirt. His eyes were surveying her speculatively. For a moment she met his gaze, then looked away nervously. She was intensely aware of his masculinity, of his sheer presence. She was also, unavoidably, remembering the feel of his arms around her and the touch of his lips on hers, and of all things, on her bare ankle. The silence between them stretched uncomfortably.

"I think my ankle is better," Carly announced at last to break the silence.

"I wouldn't recommend traipsing around this neck of the woods in heels like that," Brad pointed out.

"I think you're right."

"So you run a gallery down in the city," Brad observed.

"I'm half-owner. We call it The Gallery. It's not a real art gallery. We buy and sell Americana. You know, antiques and stuff like that. Mainly to decorators."

"Up here on a buying expedition?"

Carly nodded. "How'd you guess?"

"Buyers are not an unknown breed around here."

"So you've had a lot of experience turning them down?"

Brad chuckled. His smile was open, uninhibited, and seemed to fill the showroom with sunlight. "Throwing them out is more like it. That fat sl . . . that portly gentleman who left as you arrived is a dealer. He runs a tourist trap down in the Catskills. One of those joints that sells everything from one-hundred-percent maple syrup to ceramic Swiss chalets made in Singapore. Wanted me to turn out a cheap line of woodpeckers and chickadees or some such nonsense."

"You didn't throw me out," Carly observed. "Didn't you know I was a buyer?"

"Not at first. And anyway, I only throw out the ugly ones."

"Do you do business with the ones you don't throw out?"

"No."

Carly opened her mouth to argue with him, then shut it again. He'd made his position perfectly clear, after all. Still, his works could give The Gallery a tremendous boost. For six months now, she and Fred, her partner, had been trying to build a clientele. What they really needed was a good hook, something that would get them some attention, especially from the established decorators, before their capital ran out. Somehow she had to get this man to change his mind.

"Actually, I was sorry to see you go," he continued.

Carly felt a surge of pleasure. "So how long have you been building canoes?" she asked.

"About ten years."

"Do you work alone?"

"Yes. And no, I am not married."

"I didn't ask that!" Carly protested, irritated at the way he seemed able to read her mind.

"Are you married?" he asked.

Not knowing what to say, she studied her fingernails.

"Separated?" he asked finally.

Carly nodded. "Sort of. Only we—Jason and I—were never exactly married. I'd rather not talk about it," she finished lamely.

"Okay," he agreed easily.

Mentally, Carly had been making some computations. Ten years meant he was probably thirty or so. And never married? She looked at him, trying not to let her calculations show in her eyes. He didn't look gay. But sometimes the most intensely macho types were. Then she remembered the way they'd kissed and knew beyond any doubt that he was not gay. She was suddenly powerfully aware of him as a man. It frightened her a little—and excited her a lot.

"You still want to see how I build canoes, or was that just a ploy to try to coerce me into selling you carvings?"

"It wasn't a ploy!" Carly shot back, hurt he would even think it.

"So come on, and I'll show you around," he offered, holding out his hand. When she let him help her up, it felt as if there was an energy flow from him to her, raising her temperature and making her more alert and alive to everything around her—the colors and shapes and the smells and especially the feel of his strong hand engulfing hers.

"That's a canoe?" she asked in surprise when he showed her. It was long and low and narrow, made of plastic so thin the light shone right through it. It had a few lightweight aluminum tubes to maintain its shape and molded plastic seats contoured to fit a person's bottom.

"It's a racing canoe. What did you expect?"

"Birch bark," she retorted. "No, not really, but something that looks like a canoe—an Old Town or a Grumman. It's beautiful! Is it fast?"

"Reasonably."

Their tour was interrupted by a knock at the door. It turned out to be Brad's friend, a husky, bearded blond hulk with a soft voice. The fan belt dangled casually from his big fingers almost as if it were an afterthought.

"Carly, this is Joe Johnson. Carly Meadows," Brad introduced casually.

"Hi," Carly said timidly, overwhelmed by the two massive specimens of masculinity. "Do you canoe, too?" she asked, saying the first thing that popped into her head.

"I used to."

"Used to?" Carly asked curiously.

Joe's smile was wry, but not self-pitying. "Motorcycle accident," he explained succinctly, rapping his left leg with his knuckles. There was a hollow knocking sound. "Makes the portages a bit tough."

"I would imagine," Carly replied, trying to be as casual and matter-of-fact as Joe was.

"Brad doesn't let a person off the hook easily, though. Now he makes me chase him down the river with Gatorade. Gotta run. Nice meeting you."

"What did he mean 'chase him down the river with Gatorade'?" Carly asked as she watched Joe skillfully avoid the potholes as he drove away.

"During long races, you have to have someone follow you on shore and give you supplies."

"Why can't you just take what you need with you?"

"Too heavy."

Half an hour later, Brad had the fan belt on Carly's car,

and the battery was charged up, thanks to jumper cables
from his towering, muscular four-wheel-drive station wagon.
Carly tried her car, and the motor fired up on the first try.
When the alternator light winked out, she felt both relieved
and disappointed.

"Where you headed now?" Brad asked, leaning on the
top of the Pinto, towering over her.

"Know any good motels?"

"There's a nice one, not too expensive, on the other side
of Otego."

"Where's Otego?"

"Go back to Route Seven, then hang a left. Otego's about
three miles. Just keep on going, and you'll see a small motel
on the left. It's about two or three miles from the only light
in Otego."

"Thanks," she responded, reaching for the shift lever.
"And thanks for the help, the fan belt, and everything. You
sure I don't owe you anything?"

"Oh, you do," he answered, grinning. "But I don't think
you're ready to meet my terms."

"Oh, really? Care to try me?"

"I'd love to try you," he responded softly. "That's my
terms."

"Oh!" Carly felt as if she'd been punched in the gut. "I
asked for that one, didn't I?"

"Yep. You going to be around long?"

"A few days."

"Maybe I'll see you."

"Maybe," she agreed, putting the car in gear.

Suddenly he reached in and curled one big, strong hand
around the back of her neck. Tilting his head to fit it in the
window of the car, he kissed her. Once again he was bold,
provocative, and hungry, and easily overcame her token
resistance.

"Oh yes, I'll see you again," he promised as he backed
away from the car. "I'll see you."

Chapter Two

THE MOTEL BRAD had directed her to was a cozy little family-run place shaded by towering maple trees. The rooms were set in a shallow v, the focus of which was a two-story house that held the motel office as well as the family who owned it. Counting the distance on the back roads, it was a good ten miles from Brad's workshop. From the window of her room, Carly could see a small swimming pool sparkling invitingly in the afternoon sun. For a moment she toyed with the idea of playing hooky, then sighed and picked up the telephone to place a call to her partner.

"Well, what have you found? Is this line secure? Is it a party line or anything?" Fred demanded.

If it had been anyone but Fred, she would have been sure he was kidding and laughed aloud. But to Frederick Witherspoon the Third—a Yale man who believed firmly in his college—being an antique dealer meant combining savvy business dealing with CIA-like maneuvering to acquire pieces before the competition did. Carly felt he was a little paranoid in his fear of being outbid on something. And he had no sense of humor at all.

"I'm at a small inn just off the main trade route between Istanbul and Belgrade," she whispered hoarsely. "Use Code C. I'm being followed."

"Carly, stop it," Fred protested irritably. "I'm serious. You know how important this trip is to The Gallery. I figure we have maybe six months more, at the outside, if we don't do something. We need customers, and to get them we need things that will catch the eye of some of the fey decorators."

Carly put her feet on the bed, toed off her shoes, and wriggled her toes happily. Her ankle ached, reminding her of how the afternoon had gone. Desperately, she wrenched her mind off that memory before it made rational thought impossible.

"I made one find, but it didn't work out."

14

"What sort of a find?" Fred asked.

"I spotted a carving in a hardware store window and stopped in to ask about it. Turned out to be made by a local," she explained.

"What sort of carving?"

Remembering it, Carly felt a twinge of regret that the owner hadn't been willing to sell. A twinge? Convulsion was more like it. She wanted that piece for herself—so badly she could taste it. "It was a fox, carved out of maple."

"Was it any good?"

"Magnificent."

"So, what happened?" Fred pressed.

"The owner wouldn't sell, at any price."

"I hope you didn't offer too much," Fred cautioned. "We don't want people getting the idea we're made of money."

"Not too much," she assured him, being deliberately vague.

"What about the artist? Did you find the artist?"

"I found the artist. No go."

"What do you mean no go?"

Sliding her free hand under her thick shoulder-length curls, she lifted them off the back of her neck and let the air conditioning cool her. "He's not interested."

"How much did you offer him?"

"We never got that far. But I made it plain we could make it worth his while."

"Why didn't you get that far?" Fred asked suspiciously.

"It just didn't feel right," Carly answered. Somehow, she was almost certain an outright cash offer would have gotten her tossed out on her ear.

Fred sighed disgustedly. "Carly, how many times have I told you that money talks in this business? If you can't get down to brass tacks, we'll never get anywhere. Artists are always hungry, and they always respond to cash offers."

"Brad Weston didn't seem very hungry to me," Carly snapped. Brad was definitely hungry, she mused to herself, but not in the way Fred meant. She twirled her finger in a lock of her hair, dwelling pleasurably on the sensations Brad had triggered in her. Then she realized Fred had asked her a question and she'd missed it.

"I asked you what he does for a living," Fred repeated, his tone loaded with frustration.

"He makes canoes."

There was a pregnant silence. "Canoes?" Fred responded at last, as if he'd never heard of them.

"He makes paddles, too. He has a shop where he sells them, and wood-burning stoves and bicycles and cross-country skis and stuff like that."

"Sounds like a general store. Where are you, anyway?"

"Little town called Otego, about halfway between Binghamton and Albany."

"Why so far north? We agreed that the Catskills were the place to go hunting," he pointed out.

"Do you have any idea of the prices in resorts like Hunter and Windham? I didn't until I looked. Anyway, this is much more rural," she explained. "Farming country, instead of resorts."

"Sounds like hicksville," Fred commented sourly.

"That's on Long Island," she retorted. "This is a beautiful place. Lovely rolling hills, all green and rich. Really gorgeous. And the village is nice. Lots of old Victorian mansions."

"Thanks for the travelogue, but place of origin—beautiful or not—has no influence on what people pay for things," he reminded her. "So what are you going to do now? You're not going to give up on this guy if he's as good as you say he is."

"I don't know what more I can do. He was quite firm. As a matter of fact, he'd just run off another dealer. Bombarded the poor guy with clay cannonballs."

Carly realized that she was desperately hoping Fred would come up with some excuse for her to see Brad. Then she remembered Brad's promise that he would see her again, and her spirits rose and she forgot Fred. Lifting her hair over the back of the chair, she slid down until she could rest her head on the back.

"Any other prospects?" Fred pressed.

"I thought I'd hang around, check out the local shops, and see what else turns up. There are a couple of antique places in town that might have something."

"Well, watch what you pay. And try to haggle for a change, will you?"

Carly sighed. She'd gotten a top-notch education in haggling from the owner of the secondhand furniture store she'd worked in. That was something they didn't teach at Yale. "Okay, boss."

"I'm not your boss, I'm your partner," he said acidly.

"I'll check in again soon," she said tiredly. Not wanting to get into a pointless discussion with him on long distance, she hung up before he could say anything.

Getting to her feet, she walked over to the window and eyed the pool. She should be out checking out the antique stores. She'd seen two or three in Otego alone, and heaven knew what she might turn up in Oneonta, the nearest large town.

But it was late, she told herself. No one was in a mood to do business this late in the afternoon. And anyway, the stores probably weren't even open.

Which gave her an excuse to dig into her suitcase for her bathing suit. She held up the wisp of maillot dubiously. Skin tight, it was fine for Fire Island, but a bit daring for the boonies. She considered not going swimming . . . Then the glitter of the pool caught her eye and decided her.

Once changed, she paused, sucked in her tummy, and studied her reflection in the bathroom mirror. Not bad for twenty-eight, she mused. She had to watch it or she got "potty." But at five feet two, she still had what had caught Jason's interest during that art class at Cooper Union. Lots of swimming at the Y had kept her relatively firm, at least.

Her dark, almost black, eyes made a striking contrast to her thick, wavy auburn hair. And thanks to a few invitations out to Fire Island and some forays to Riverside Park, she'd managed a tan that was a credit to the Shawnee branch of her family. Turning away from the mirror, she headed for the pool.

Only after she got there did she realize the pool was in full view of the main road. Nervously, feeling self-conscious, she moved a chaise around to block a little of the view from the highway.

Sitting on the side of the pool with her feet dangling in the water, she tucked her thick hair into her bathing cap. Then, tipping forward, she rolled into the cool, clear chlorine-scented water, letting her momentum carry her down and across the pool. It felt as if the water was sweeping off all the dirt and sweat left by the long drive.

With no one there to intrude, she began swimming slow,

nonstop laps, feeling her muscles ripple and stretch and flex with relief at the exercise. The steady rhythm gave her mind plenty of time to wander back to Fred and The Gallery.

And, not for the first time she wondered just how smart it had been to link up with him. He had his Yale education and a kind of surface gloss, but he combined it with an arrogance that could be irritating. Not, she mused, that he was as bad as Jason. Now there had been a colossal mistake. It was easy to look back now and see how she'd gotten involved with Jason. A different sort of involvement, of course.

The relationship had been a direct result of her rebellious phase. She'd run away from home, fled Iowa and what she felt were its stuffy, conservative Bible belt attitudes, and gone to New York City. She was going to be an artist, unfettered by the conventional rules that bound everyone else. She was going to be sophisticated and successful and escape her country hick roots.

Reality, in the form of the need for money, had finally driven her to model for art classes while she tried to acquire the education she'd neglected. Jason, one of the teaching associates, had taken an interest in her, and his style had been just the thing to ensnare her, thanks to her Iowa naïveté. He lived in Greenwich Village. He was creative, daring, and an intellectual. He was an idealist. His interest had been flattering and exciting.

Posing for him had been anything but the impersonal, passionless thing it had been for the classes. Posing for a horde of strangers, she'd felt as romantic as a side of beef. Jason had made it much more—*exciting* was the acceptably descriptive word she came up with as she reached the end of the pool. Sucking in a deep breath, she pushed off and started another lap.

Thinking back on it now, it all seemed grubby and sordid, but still wildly romantic, too. She'd loved him, of course. She'd loved him for his intellectual ferment, his sexual passion. There had been long, wine-sodden bull sessions lasting late into the night.

It had been, she reflected as she let her feet sink to the bottom in the shallow end of the pool, a very exciting time. Stripping off her bathing cap, she shook her hair out as she climbed the steps and made her way to the chaise. The warm breeze dried her, raising goosebumps until she blotted herself with the towel. Stretching out on the lounge, she tilted her face to the setting sun and let her hair dangle back over the end of the chaise so the air could dry the damp ends.

She really had expected that she and Jason would get married eventually. In fact, she had thought of them as married. Who needed a silly piece of paper to prove the permanency of their love? They were modern idealists. They were committed to each other, had a meaningful relationship, so what else did they need?

She had found out just how deeply Jason was committed to ideals and to her when she'd accidentally found out the class he'd supposedly been taking at the New School didn't exist. The class had turned out to be named Judy, and she hadn't had a thing to do with the New School.

After a lot of screaming about honesty and openness and possessiveness, Carly had left, her clothes stuffed in a bulging laundry bag, her spider plant clutched to her bosom. Later that night, as she had lain down on the sofa in a friend's apartment, the tears had come. It had all suddenly become sickeningly sordid and decadent, and she had felt soiled and used and stupid.

Opening her eyes, Carly gazed at the slowly dying waves in the pool. She'd rejected Iowa, with its churchgoing Sundays and corn fields, for a shabby studio apartment in Greenwich Village. Then she'd rejected that, too, and moved uptown. She'd gone for respectability and sophistication, as much as her budget allowed.

With her lack of salable skills, she'd had a hard time finding anything and had finally managed to land a job in a used furniture store. It had paid the rent—barely—and let her keep dreaming of being a real artist until she'd come to the gloomy conclusion she wasn't good enough. It was one thing to be able to draw well. It was another to make simple sketches into a salable art form. And she had also reached the conclusion that it might be exciting to be an artist, but that part of the excitement was hair-breadth escapes from starvation.

It was at about that time that Fred had come on the scene. He'd been searching for a nineteenth-century railroad lantern to use as a ceiling light for his apartment. Intrigued by the

challenge of the search and—though she didn't like to admit
it to herself—impressed by his degree from Yale, Carly
had joined him in burrowing through endless piles of dusty
relics, to no avail. Almost simultaneously, they'd come to
the realization that there might be a need to be met here.

A perusal of a dozen similar shops convinced them that
there was no one who specialized in Americana. There was
a market, they thought, for all sorts of native American
relics as decorator items. Perhaps a rusty antique apple peel-
er-corer was just the thing to add a "homey" touch to a
modern kitchen in a twenty-story high-rise. Maybe someone's quarter-million-dollar condo was just crying for a genuine chamber pot.

After finally locating the lantern at a flea market in lower
Manhattan, she and Fred had sat down together and hashed
things over. He, it turned out, had some business courses
in addition to those in his major—art history. And he was
fed up with his job at a Fifty-Seventh Street art gallery.

In the course of her work at the furniture store, Carly
had found she had a shrewd eye for value. She had also
discovered she really enjoyed the horse trading and haggling
that went on in the secondhand business. Frustratingly, the
only time she got to do it was when her boss was out.

But the discussion with Fred would have come to nothing
if it hadn't been for Carly's maternal great-grandmother.
Much to the entire family's surprise, something of value
had turned up when her house was being remodeled for
Carly's brother and his wife. Her husband, it seemed, had
taken a flier on an obscure stock that had turned out to be
a winner. And there was an attached letter that left the stock
to Carly.

It had seemed an incredible stroke of fate. By himself,
Fred hadn't had the capital he needed to start his own business. Then all of a sudden Carly had money. So she provided
half the capital and the street smarts, while Fred supplied
the business knowledge and the polish of his Ivy League
background. And thanks to his time at the art gallery, he
was an expert on how to set up eye-catching displays and
on how to impress customers.

Unfortunately, so far it wasn't enough, and their capital
was disappearing rapidly. Which was the reason for her trip
upstate. Fred hoped she'd turn up something really dramatic

they could billboard to get the attention he felt they needed. Carly had gone along with the plan, more because she was hoping to stretch their remaining money a little farther by picking up some decent pieces at prices lower than what she'd have to pay at the city's flea markets, pawn shops, auctions, and secondhand shops than because she thought it was likely she'd find some incredible treasure at a low price.

"When I said I'd see you, I had no idea I'd see this much of you," someone said from the gate in the fence around the pool. "All this time I've been wasting myself carving woodchuck and fox. What I should have been doing was immortalizing you in wood."

Just the sound of Brad Weston's voice was enough to make Carly's heart do flip-flops. Determined not to show surprise or the pleasure she felt, she rolled her head languidly and looked over at him. "What are you doing here?"

"Looking for you. I am, it seems, unexpectedly successful."

"Enjoying the view?" she inquired brightly.

"Very much," he said candidly. Somehow she didn't mind his appreciative study the way she generally did men ogling her.

"Flattery will get you nowhere, but keep talking—I love it."

"How about brightening my evening by having dinner with me?"

"Okay," she agreed promptly. In the first place, she hadn't been looking forward to a meal alone. In the second, Brad Weston's company was not something she had any desire to avoid. And in the third, she told herself virtuously, she owed it to Fred and The Gallery to try to change Brad's mind.

"You want to go like that?" he asked, surveying her with obvious relish as she got to her feet. "It would certainly cause a stir at McDonald's."

"McDonald's?" she asked as he stepped aside to let her pass. He circled his hand around her waist, ushering her by. She liked his touch and answered the gleam in his eye with a questioning lift of one eyebrow.

"Well, you just told me flattery would get me nowhere, so I figured why bother to try bribery."

Carly laughed. She enjoyed the deft twists his mind kept taking. "Why don't you give it a try?" she suggested, shooting him a deliberately flirtatious look over her shoulder.

"Will it work?" he asked as she unlocked her door.

"You'll have to wait and see," she teased. "And anyway, it depends on the size of the bribe." When he tried to follow her into the room, she restrained him with a hand on his chest. "Sorry, but the bathroom in this place is so small you have to step outside just to change your mind."

"Seems to me I've already seen everything," he countered.

"Not quite," she said, closing the door between them. "I'll only be a minute."

"Hurry," he urged. "I wither, separated as I am from your glowing presence."

"I'll bet," she retorted as she rummaged desperately through her suitcase. Blast! What the devil did she have with her that would be right? Even if it hadn't gotten dirty when she'd fallen in his driveway, she couldn't wear the same skirt and blouse she'd had on earlier.

Hoping he didn't have any place too formal in mind, she settled on a white peasant blouse with a daringly low neckline and a pair of stretch jeans. As her mother would put it, they were tight enough to show she was a woman but loose enough to show she was a lady. For jewelry she wore the elk tooth her great-grandmother had given her. Suspended from a fine gold chain, the yellowed ivory glowed against her tanned skin, a beautiful, primitive symbol, one that she had always treasured. The tooled sandals she wore were the result of a trip she'd taken to New Mexico. Not wanting to take the time for a lot of makeup, she made do with just a touch of lipstick.

"You still there?" she asked as she hastily brushed her hair, the bristles snapping through her thick auburn mane, the heavy waves caressing her shoulders. A jade barrette kept it from spilling over one eye à la Rhonda Fleming.

"Faint with hunger and pining for a glimpse of you," he called.

"Sounds like we're back to flattery," she commented as she grabbed a sweater and purse and headed for the door. When she yanked it open, Brad fell inward in a mock faint, draping his arms over her shoulders, pushing her back a pace before he caught himself and her. She drove her palms against his delectably hard chest and held him off.

"Worked when you did it," he grumbled. "How about a little mouth-to-mouth resuscitation?"

"How about a little dinner?" she countered.

"Man does not live by bread alone," he pointed out as she closed the door and checked the lock had caught.

"First things first."

"Does that mean if I feed you, you will?" he asked hopefully as he opened the door of his towering station wagon for her.

"It does not," she answered firmly.

"Oh. How about steak?"

"Sounds great."

At the third light they came to, Carly eyed the Burger King on the opposite corner, then shot Brad a sharp questioning look. He shook his head, smiled, and hung a left. When he turned in at a worn parking lot in front of what looked like a factory, she wondered what he was up to.

The restaurant, tucked in a corner of the old factory, was dark and cool. He led her past a bar jammed with a raucous crowd and into a small, pleasant dining room. It was all wood paneled and orange lighted, the air lively with the scent of garlic and charcoal. In a few minutes, they had menus and their drinks were on the way.

"I still don't understand why you're not interested in my offer," Carly noted hesitantly after they'd ordered—and wondered if she should have left the subject until later.

Brad immediately looked irritated and closed up. "Are we going to talk business?"

"Makes the dinner deductible," Carly pointed out, cursing herself for sticking her foot in it.

"Since I'm paying, not unless we talk canoes," he countered.

"Okay," Carly agreed lightly. "Why do you build canoes?"

"It's a living," he answered, swizzling his Scotch in his glass.

"Can't be a very good one."

"How would you know?"

"I don't. But I do know your carvings would sell. I can't believe you aren't interested in increasing your income,"

Carly argued. She sipped her Dubonnet on the rocks and smiled knowingly at him over the rim of her glass. "Fred— my partner—reminded me that every man has his price," she teased.

"Bribery might work on you, but it won't on me," Brad answered, smiling back. She liked the way it made his dark eyes sparkle.

"I never said it would work on me," she corrected.

"I said might," he pointed out. "Who's Fred?"

"I told you. My partner in The Gallery," she said, intrigued by the hint of jealousy in the question.

"What's he like?"

"He's all right," she answered vaguely. "He's got a degree in art history from Yale."

"A Yalie? Poor fellow. Poor you!"

"Why poor me?" Carly asked.

"How could a sweet young thing like you get mixed up with a Yalie, of all things?"

"Did you go to Harvard or something?"

"Princeton, actually."

"You're kidding!"

"Nope. So, what else has Fred done besides pick the wrong college?"

"He was working as assistant manager of a gallery on Fifty-seventh Street, and I was working in a secondhand furniture store. He came in looking for something for his apartment, and we wound up searching for it together. Then I came into a bit of an inheritance, and we decided to combine our resources."

"And you're just good friends?" Brad asked skeptically.

"As a matter of fact, we're not even that. We're business partners," Carly retorted. "Fred concentrates on Vassar and Bryn Mawr graduates."

"So what's a nice girl like you doing raiding the countryside for antiques like Attila the Hun?"

Carly glared at him. "What do you mean, raiding the countryside like Attila the Hun?"

"You think you're the first New York City dealer to discover our heritage?" he asked wryly. "I've seen this area raided by sharks from the city. They come up here, pockets bulging with cash, and proceed to strip us of our history. They'd sell their own grandmothers if they could make a profit on it. It's just like bootlegging Aztec artifacts out of Mexico or raiding the tombs of Egyptian pharaohs."

Carly felt her Irish temper rising. "Listen, buster, if you're trying to get on my good side, this is not the way to do it."

"My, my, I must have struck a raw nerve," Brad responded blandly.

"Well, I'm not about to sit here and let you characterize me as a grave robber, of all things," Carly pointed out. "The shoe doesn't fit, and I'm not about to wear it."

"Okay, Cinderella . . ."

"Prince Charming you ain't."

"Never said I was."

"Well, you're right about that, at least!" Pushing the ice around in her glass, Carly studied him speculatively. "As long as we're being rude, what's a Princetonian doing up here in the middle of nowhere? And you'll note I did not refer to you as a gentleman from Princeton."

"Building canoes," he answered with a twinkle in his eye.

"Funny," Carly responded wryly, making a face at him. "No, I mean why are you here—uh—in Otego? . . ."

"Why aren't I down in the city designing great bridges or housing for the masses? Princeton in the nation's service and all that?"

"I think that's what I mean."

"I almost did," Brad admitted. "I came that close." He held up his thumb and finger pressed together.

Something about the way he said it gave Carly a chill. There was something so intense buried there she wasn't sure she wanted it unearthed. At the same time, curiosity drove her on. "What happened?" she asked warily.

Brad's face clouded over in thought. "Well, about the time I was ready to graduate, I was faced with some tough decisions. I didn't want to go on to grad school. I was fed up with studying. I had the usual bunch of interviews with the recruiters that came on campus. I even talked with the man from the CIA."

"Good grief!" Carly imagined Brad as a spy, and that image really scared her.

"That idea bit the dust when they told me I'd have to go through Marine Corps boot camp," Brad admitted wryly. "Anyway, I explored a lot of different possibilities. I had interviews on campus with half a dozen different outfits.

"I don't know how it is at other colleges, but at Princeton they use a screening system—give a preliminary interview on campus, and then if you're both still interested, you move on to meeting with them at their own offices.

"I was interested enough in a couple of the outfits to go on with them. But somewhere along the line, it all started to go sour for me. One firm asked me up to their skyscraper on Park Avenue. We came out of the elevator and there was about ten acres of gray carpeting dotted with desks. The personnel man led me over to a desk and said this was where I'd be working if they offered me the job. I was afraid I wouldn't be able to find my desk in the morning! They all looked the same. I probably would have had to put a daisy on a tall stem on it or something, like finding your Volkswagen in a shopping-mall parking lot.

"There were a couple of other possibilities like that. I spent three solid days interviewing with one firm. But in the end we came to a mutual understanding."

"So what happened?"

He frowned. "I was offered a job . . ."

"And?"

"I came to my senses, realized I wanted that kind of job about as badly as I wanted root canal work," he answered pensively. "I'd been bull . . . uh . . . kidding myself, and them. I'm not a company man, and never could be. I just didn't fit that mold.

"And I didn't want to be a commuter, either. I'd seen my own father commute two hours a day to a desk job. Or rather, I hadn't seen my father, since he was on the train before I got up and I was being tucked in bed just about the time he got home.

"So I quit fooling myself, quit trying to be something I wasn't. I told them thanks, but no thanks. Nothing personal and all that, but it's just not for me. They were very nice about it, considering all the time they'd wasted on me."

"Why didn't you make up your mind a little sooner?"

"I should have. I think one reason was that it was the route my parents wanted me to take, and I didn't want to disappoint them—kept telling myself it couldn't be as bad as I thought it'd be—that I'd like it if I tried it.

"Dad was amazingly understanding about the whole thing.

It was almost as if he wished he'd had the nerve to do what I did—but he grew up during the Depression, and jobs were hard to come by then. If you had one, you hung onto it whether you liked it or not. I'm afraid my mother never has forgiven me. I think she always had this image of her son, the Ivy League graduate, as a corporate president. I still feel badly about disappointing her."

"I know the feeling," Carly said, remembering all the fights with her mother—who had been positive marriage to a farmer and lots of children were what Carly should want in life. When she'd begun to live with Jason, her mother had quit writing and wouldn't even come to the phone. "Why didn't you want a normal job? You wouldn't have stayed in the huge room long. No job starts out all wonderful and glamorous."

"I'm not sure. General cussedness, probably. Though I'm sure my grandfather's example had a lot to do with it."

"Why?" Carly asked, fascinated by the parallels she saw between herself and Brad. She'd had her great-grandmother, Brad his grandfather.

"He was a stone cutter, from Greece. When I was little, I once watched him build a pair of gateposts for some rich family. The posts were granite. He started work at seven-thirty every morning. He shaped each block with his hammer and chisels, as carefully as if he were building the Taj Mahal. He'd lift each block into place to check the fit, time after time, and those blocks weighed seventy, eighty pounds or more.

"Down the street, some union masons were working on the same sort of thing. They'd get there about nine, start work around nine-thirty, take a coffee break at eleven, an hour for lunch, and knock off at four-thirty. There were, oh, I don't know, three or four of them. One to chisel, one to mix mortar, two to lift, something like that. Grampa didn't have much use for them, I'm afraid."

Fascinated, Carly listened intently.

"Anyway, when my grandfather was done, the only way you could tell his posts from the ones he was matching at the other end of the circular drive was that the stone he'd used wasn't weathered yet. When he was done, he'd made something that was all his. He left something behind he could be proud of, that he could point to as being all his work. He'd done his best, and he didn't have to share either the credit or the blame with anyone else. Maybe it was all for nothing, I don't know. It wasn't—isn't—a matter of choice. He wasn't a team player, and neither am I."

Carly had to shake herself to draw back from the depths of his soul. "Integrity means a great deal to you, doesn't it?"

"I guess so."

"Do you like living up here in the wilderness?" she asked, feeling it was time to change the subject.

"You going to try and make me believe you're a city girl?" he asked, grinning.

"Uh, no," Carly admitted. "Iowa, as a matter of fact. Near Des Moines. How'd you know?"

"You can take the girl out of Iowa, but . . ."

"... You can't take Iowa out of the girl," she finished with him. "Does it show that much?" She was surprised. Most people took her for the big city sophisticate she tried to be. He seemed to be able to see more deeply into her than anyone she'd ever met before.

Brad smiled. "In spite of your chic city clothes, you've got the corn-fed good looks and *joie de vivre* of a farm girl."

"Oh, yuck!"

"What? You'd rather have the sallowness of the city?"

"You make me sound like a hick!"

"I didn't mean it that way," he assured her, sitting back so the waitress could serve him. "I meant it as a compliment. And you don't seem like an antique dealer. Which is also supposed to be a compliment."

"Then thank you, I guess."

"How's your steak?" Brad asked as he sliced into his.

"The steak is fine, it's the conversation I'm having some trouble with," Carly grumbled.

"Doesn't seem to have ruined your appetite," he observed as she attacked her steak enthusiastically.

"The thing I can't understand," Carly noted over dessert, "is why someone with talent and an education like yours doesn't apply it to something meaningful."

"You sound like a frustrated artist," he observed shrewdly.

"I suppose I am," Carly admitted, staring morosely into her coffee.

"What sort of work do you do?"

Carly frowned and then sighed. "Oh, I used to sketch some."

"So what happened?" Brad asked with gentle sympathy.

"No matter how hard I worked, my drawings didn't seem good enough," she admitted. "I never seemed to go deeper, beyond the basic mechanical skill—which I came by naturally. It was a matter of development, I guess. And I knew I'd never make a living at it."

"Selling isn't everything," he pointed out.

"It is if you want to eat."

"So you gave up."

She glared at him. "At least I tried."

"Meaning that I haven't?"

"Well, you're sure not using the talent God gave you the way you should be," she said bitterly.

"And you've sold out and are eating at the expense of other people's heirlooms and family treasures," Brad retorted.

"Now, wait a minute!"

"You think I don't know how the racket works? You latch on to some poor sucker who's down on his luck, pay him a pittance for his irreplaceable family heirlooms, and then sell them to someone who doesn't care about anything except something green to fill that blank wall behind the sofa or a knick-knack to impress the boss's wife when she comes for dinner."

Carly glared at him and knew she was dangerously near the boiling point. "Now look, Mister Holier-than-Thou . . ."

"And I'm not even touching on the forgeries or stolen works foisted off on the public," he plowed on inexorably.

"Now, you wait just a damn minute!" Carly exploded.

"Something wrong?" Brad asked with bland innocence.

"I'll tell you what's wrong," Carly snapped. "You've got an absolutely classical case of bleeding-heart-liberal ignorant arrogance. Boy, you characters make my blood boil! I have never known anyone so willing to jump to stupid conclusions as you are. You're egotistical, arrogant, rude, unreliable, egocentric, and totally impractical, to say nothing of bull-headed and boorish."

Brad sat back in his chair and looked at her as if she were a pet that had suddenly turned on and bitten him.

"I'll tell you for truly true, Mr. Weston," Carly plowed

on. "Any profit we make doesn't make up for the aggravation of having to put up with people like you. If I never see you again, it'll be too soon!"

"Darn!" Brad griped with a smile that totally disarmed her.

"What?" Carly squeaked, floundering at the abrupt shift.

Brad leaned across the table, his hand capturing hers before she could draw it back. It felt as if she'd been touched by a live wire. She could feel all her insides melting into a pool of desire.

"I was going to ask you to come home with me," he said softly.

Chapter Three

CARLY MADE A feeble attempt to retrieve her hand from Brad's possessive grasp. "You are out of your everloving mind."

"Not everloving," he countered.

"Never loving?" Carly asked, enjoying his warm, strong grip on her.

"Never before," he answered, grinning.

"Oh wow! You really expect me to believe that?"

"Yes," he replied, suddenly serious, his eyes pinning hers.

Unnerved, Carly withdrew her hand.

Brad winked at her and reached for the change the waitress had left. After figuring the tip, he returned his attention to Carly. "You ready to go?"

"Where?" she asked suspiciously.

"My place—or yours?" Brad asked as he courteously drew her chair back. "Or we could just go park—pretend we're teenagers."

"Why is it you phrased that in such a way that no matter what I answer, I'm in trouble?"

"You expect me to make it easy for you?"

"Yes," Carly grumped lightly as they left the restaurant.

The cool evening air was heavy with vague, obscure country smells. Overhead, a few clouds were tinted salmon pink by the setting sun.

"You still haven't answered my question," Brad pointed out as she climbed into his station wagon.

"Proposition, you mean. Home, James, to my motel. Where I intend to retire alone. Solo. Singly, as in by myself."

"Any special reason? Bad breath? Offensive body odor?"

"You're going too fast. We've known each other less than twelve hours. I could ask you what you think of me, but you've already made that *quite* obvious."

"Well, just to make sure I don't misunderstand and blow it again, am I right that there's hope for the future?"

"There's always hope for the future. It's just that I'd rather you didn't treat this whole thing like a singles bar encounter."

"I'm not," he assured her as they halted at the last light on the way out of Oneonta. Ahead, the western sky was now tinged with mauve. The hills were dark, velvety shapes, bejeweled here and there on their lower slopes with the lights of houses and farms. "Problem is, I'm not sure just how long you're going to be around."

"Oh, a few days," she answered vaguely. "I'm still hoping to find some good stuff for The Gallery."

"Cheap," Brad suggested as they pulled away from the intersection.

Carly nodded. "I'm in business to make a profit. Not an outrageous one, but enough to keep the rent paid."

"So you're going to rip off the local yokels..."

"I'm going to buy things from them that would otherwise bring them nothing..."

"Except pleasure," Brad interrupted.

"And sell them to people down in the city who'll appreciate and enjoy them," she continued determinedly.

"Such altruism," Brad commented wryly. "Damn!" he swore as a shadowy form leaped in front of the car. The tires shrieked, and Carly was thrown hard against her safety belt as the station wagon slewed sideways in the road.

"What was that?" she asked unsteadily when they came to a stop.

"Deer," Brad answered curtly. "You all right?"

"Glad I buckled up," she said, relieved to have had the conversation derailed. "Does that happen often?"

"Yep. The local body shops and car dealers keep all kinds of grillwork in stock to repair the constant damage."

"What about spare parts for the deer?" Carly asked nervously, still unsettled by the encounter.

"I'm afraid they're not all as lucky as that one," Brad said as he turned in at the motel parking lot and pulled up in front of her room.

"Don't get out."

"Dream on," he chuckled as he opened his door.

"It was a lovely dinner," she assured him, suddenly feeling as shy as she had when coming home from a date in high school. She used the excuse of finding her key to avoid looking at him.

He surprised her by touching her hair gently. stroking a few strands away from her part. "You have lovely hair," he commented softly, his tone warm and intimate.

She gave a gentle toss of her head and looked up at him. "Thanks."

"You're welcome," he answered as he captured her chin in his hand and his mouth came down on hers. The touch of his lips was electrifying. Without her even willing it, her mouth responded, as did her entire body. She slid her hands up his arms and around his back to caress his shoulder blades and steely muscles. She rose up on her toes, pressing herself against him as his tongue probed past her teeth. The strength drained out of her and she sagged against him.

One of his powerful thighs nudged its way between hers, and she pressed herself against it, triggering a hot wave of pleasure. He thrust against her, his hands clutching her so hard she could feel his fingers bruising her. Her breasts were crushed against his solid chest, and she felt as if her lungs were on fire as the kiss went on and on. At last, trying to recover her equilibrium, she eased back away from him.

"Still no?" he asked hopefully.

"No," she whispered, battling her own hunger as much as his.

"You're a tough one," he observed.

"Right. I'd never crack under torture."

He chuckled, and the sound drummed through her provocatively. "Want to bet?"

She didn't answer as she fitted the key into the lock.

"I'll see you tomorrow. You'll be here?"

"Either here or in Otego at the antique stores," she answered, turning back to face him.

"I'll see you," he said softly, drawing her close again, his mouth seeking hers. Her tongue dueled with his, and once again there was that gut-wrenching contact all the way down their bodies.

Finally, she forced herself to let go. "Thanks for the dinner," she managed to say reasonably steadily.

"My pleasure," he assured her. "Good night."

"Good night," she responded, feeling a little dissatisfied that he was relenting so easily. Once in her room, the door closed between them, she leaned back against it and concentrated on keeping herself from yanking it open and calling him back. She heard his car door slam and the engine rumble to life. She felt as if she had nerve endings that reached into the parking lot, that told her the exact moment he pulled out onto the highway.

"Damn," she swore softly. Not another artist! In spite of everything he'd said, that's what he was and she knew it, even if he didn't. He had the intensity, the incredible focus, of an artist. When she was with him, she felt as if she were the only thing in his universe. It was intimidating, flattering, and dangerously exciting.

"Damn, and double damn," Carly growled as she got ready for bed. She was acutely aware of the delicious, swollen tenderness of her lips and the heavenly hunger in her loins. And the emptiness in her heart that she'd almost forgotten about. After Jason, she'd sworn she'd never again get involved with an artist. She hadn't lived a completely cloistered life since Jason, but none of the men had been more than casual dates, and none had shared her bed, though many had tried. And none of them had been artists.

Her sleep was filled with strange dreams, dreams of being a section of tree chosen by a tall, dark, handsome woodcutter and then being shaped by him, his chisels and knives molding her willing grain until she was finished and polished and brought to life to share his passions.

She awoke to bright summer sun peering through the window and hitting her in the face. Blinking against the glare, she rolled over and bit down on a mouthful of pillow as she found her watch and checked the time. It was Friday, and the antique shops beckoned. As always, it was enough to get her out of bed. She dressed quickly in a short-sleeved pale yellow blouse and trim blue slacks with a matching belt. As she decided against socks and tied her sneakers on her bare feet, she reflected that the informality of country life did have its advantages.

An hour and a half later, her fast broken at the local Burger King, she was parking her rented Pinto near the only traffic light in Otego—across the street from the school and in front of the hardware store with Brad's fox in the window.

Two doors toward Oneonta were a pair of antique shops, and one door in the opposite direction was another.

The first shop she explored was a disappointment. Not because it didn't have anything of interest, but because the owner had a shrewd knowledge of the value of his merchandise. The prices weren't out of line, but there wasn't any margin left for a profit if she paid them.

Carly thought wistfully of the endless stories she'd heard of marvelous finds in attics and barns. She recalled once meeting an expert on rare books who'd found an original copy of the Declaration of Independence. She was sure that he would go to his grave content no matter what else happened in his life.

"See anything you like?" the proprietor asked, disrupting her train of thought.

"Oh, no thanks. Or rather, I see a lot that I like, but it's not exactly what I'm in the market for." She couldn't bring herself to admit to him that she was a dealer. She suddenly realized she hadn't been thinking clearly if she expected to find bargain-basement prices in a shop like this. He needed to make a profit, just as she did.

"Which is?" The man was middle-aged, big, easygoing, with the open friendliness so rare in the city.

"Americana," Carly explained. "Paintings, statuary, antique utensils, decorator items. I'm not into furniture, really."

"Got some nice stoneware back here," he pointed out.

"Do you have anything by local artists?" she asked. Some of Brad's work had to be available somewhere.

"Not unless it's someone who's been dead for a century," he said, smiling broadly. "We've got a few dabblers around here, but no one produces anything anyone down in the city'd be interested in."

Carly flushed at the accuracy of his guess about her. "How'd you know I'm from the city?"

"It's a small town. I knew you were a stranger and took a shot in the dark," he told her, a twinkle in his eye.

"You know Brad Weston?" she asked casually.

"Name rings a bell. Don't connect him with antiques, though. Think maybe he's with the emergency squad. Something like that."

"Oh. Well, thanks anyway."

"Come back anytime," he invited as she let herself out.

Outside, she paused and glanced across the street, past the big brick school, to the rolling hills north of the village. Everything was so green. In the city, she was always surprised to discover when they dug up the pavement there was real dirt under it. Here, with their slate sidewalks, tree-lined streets, and neatly maintained lawns, the people seemed carefully protective of all living things. The air was so clear it seemed untouched.

She looked at the next place she'd planned to visit and shook her head. She was going to have to rethink her entire strategy. Obviously, these shops were not the place for her to be looking. She decided to take a walk while she puzzled it out.

With a frivolous glance at the traffic light, she crossed and looked up at a three-story wood-frame clapboard building that was, according to the neat sign, an auction house. There was a sale scheduled for Saturday. Now, that offered some possibilities. She added it to her mental agenda for the weekend.

Further along, the main street was lined with dignified nineteenth-century houses, crisply maintained, proud in their white paint, shutters, and boldly columned porches. The latter showed signs of being used the way they had been since they'd been built—as places to rock and chat and observe.

The age of the village made her sure there were some marvelous finds lurking. But no matter what Brad's cynical view of her profession was, she was not about to just boldly walk up to someone's door and ask to buy their heirloom door knocker for a pittance, for heaven's sake. Still, it was nice to dream of turning up an unknown work by Revere, for example, lost and forgotten in a musty attic.

The sidewalk was shaded by towering maples. Their leaves stirred gently in the breeze, rustling comfortingly, while cicadas sang with a metallic shrill. Someone, somewhere near, had already cut a lawn that morning. It all brought back delightful memories of her childhood. She remembered the feel of her bicycle jolting over the frost- and root-tilted blocks of sidewalk when she'd gotten old enough and bold enough to ride the mile into town from the farm. Playfully, she skipped and danced to avoid stepping on any cracks.

It wasn't enough to keep her from thinking about Brad Weston. And she found herself thinking of him as a man, rather than as an artist or a potential supplier for The Gallery—or a critic of her line of work. The man had revived sensations she'd thought she'd never feel again. She wasn't sure she was eager to be reexperiencing them. There was a certain safety in dullness.

Stumbling slightly, Carly suddenly realized she'd run out of sidewalk. Looking up, she found she'd walked right out of town. On her left was a neatly tended graveyard, and beyond that, a farm, where cows grazed contentedly. On the other side there were a few more houses, an open field, and then, in the distance, barns and silos began to loom.

After looking both ways for virtually nonexistent traffic, she crossed to the north side of the street and headed back the way she'd come. The town was peaceful, serene. An elderly lady was washing her windows, and at another house a heavily pregnant woman was contentedly weeding a garden bright with tall spears of gladioli. Behind the flowers were neatly tended vegetables—corn, and vines heavy with ripening tomatoes. Carly remembered how sweet the corn had tasted fresh out of her parents' garden. There were some things she did miss in the city, she reflected as she nodded to the woman washing her windows.

The sound of a car coming up behind her made her turn. The sight of Brad's burly four-wheel-drive wagon made her heart give an unexpected jump. She managed to restrain herself and only wave timidly as she cursed herself for the surge of joy she felt at the sight of him. Ridiculous! She'd only met him the day before, after all. She was behaving like a lovestruck teenager. And where was her vow not to get involved with another damn artist?

He slowed to a stop right in the middle of the street. "Howdy, ma'am. Yore new in town, ain't ya?" he drawled. "Must be the new schoolmarm."

"Hi," she responded, feeling both excited and shy. Why was it, she wondered, she always had the feeling she had his entire attention, as if no one else in the world existed for him when he was with her?

"Busy?" he asked as she crossed to stand by his door, oblivious of the fact that she was in the middle of the street.

"Not really. What are you doing?" His car was so tall,

his face was on a level with hers. For a moment she had a silly, heart-quickening impulse to lean in the window and kiss his oh-so-kissable lips. She managed to curb it.

"Well, I could say I was coming down to the post office to get my mail," he answered. Someone honked impatiently, and he waved casually and angled his car over to the curb so they could pass. Carly followed when the way was clear.

"But you have a mailbox," Carly pointed out. "Set on a post carved into the most whimsical rabbit I've ever seen."

"You noticed!"

"It was hard to miss. So you weren't coming to town for your mail?"

"Nope."

"A new chisel from the hardware store?"

"Nope."

"A quart of milk from the grocery?" she guessed, feeling delightfully young and happy and silly.

"Passed that a mile back."

"I've got it! You've come to town for a shootout with the local bad guy."

"Yup, that's it. So, any luck on your buying?"

"Not a bit, you'll be glad to know." She wondered if he was going to invite her to join him. "You've got some sharp dealers around here."

"Hop in," he invited at last, to her relief. "Where'd you try?"

"Down by the hardware store. That nice-looking shop with the wood trim stained brown."

"Burt's? He's the smartest dealer in the county. Honest and fair, but he isn't a fool. And if he knew you were a buyer from the city, you didn't have a chance."

"He did, and I didn't," Carly admitted ruefully as she fastened her seat belt. "And I also made the brilliant deduction that I'm not going to find wholesale prices in a retail store."

"I think I've got just the yokel for you," Brad said, grinning. "You want bargains, you've got to get off the beaten track."

"But the only tracks I know around here are the beaten ones and the one to your house, which is hardly beaten, now that I think about it."

"That's why you need a clever, suave, debonair, and

daring great white hunter as your guide."

"You?"

"Very astute of you to notice," he said, taking a left just outside town and heading north past a sawmill. Its yard was piled high with loads of logs, stacks of lumber, and mountains of sawdust.

In a few minutes they had left behind what could have been suburbs almost anywhere. The land was open and flat, ringed by wooded hills. Apparently, judging by the tall corn flanking the road, it was good bottomland, rich and fertile. The lower slopes of the hills were pasture, grazed by herds of cows. Here and there the land had been abandoned and was slowly returning to scrub brush, hawthorn, and white pine.

"This is the most gorgeous countryside," Carly commented, surveying the graceful curves of the hills.

"I love it. Wouldn't want to live anywhere else."

"I can see why."

A few minutes more and they were headed over the hills on a paved but potholed road. Crossing through a saddle in a ridge, they headed down into another watershed. As they dove into the valley, Brad chose a dirt side road. Carly clenched her teeth as they rattled over jarring craters, scattering a flock of mourning doves at one point. A rabbit burst out of the weeds, fled along the road, and darted back into the brush with a flick of its white tail. Trees closed in around them, forming a mysterious, gloomy tunnel. Deep in the shade there were dapples of sunshine.

"You sure you're not lost?" Carly asked as the woods opened out again to abandoned pastures. They passed a barn sagging slowly into ruin.

"Yep," Brad assured her. "But I might run out of gas," he teased, shooting her a lusty glance.

His eyes tracked down her trim sleeveless yellow shirt to the dark blue slacks hugging her thighs. How was it that just the way he looked at her could make her insides go all wobbly and weak?

"Keep your eyes on the road," she scolded, squirming in her seat.

"And my hands on the wheel?"

"Definitely!"

Soon they were climbing into the hills again, and woods

closed in on either side. The air smelled of leaf mold and
growing things. A squirrel darted up a tree as they rounded
a curve. Then they were back out in the open, flanked by
weedy pastures behind tumbled-down stone walls. The wheels
grated on gravel as they slowed suddenly, then turned up
into a driveway steeper and more rugged than Brad's. The
nose of the station wagon rocked as, the gears grinding,
they lurched upward.

"Wow! Looks like something out of Faulkner or Taylor
Caldwell," Carly observed as they jounced to a halt in front
of a weathered old house.

At some distant time in the past it had been painted,
judging by the few flecks of white still clinging to the warped
clapboards. There were clotheslines strung between the porch
posts. Several pairs of overalls and a threadbare set of drop-
seat long johns dangled in the warm air. They were as gray
as the siding on the house. Whoever lived here hadn't discovered a bleach that made things whiter than white.

"Or John Steinbeck," Brad noted as he switched off the
engine.

The man who emerged from the house looked as old and
seasoned as his dwelling. Short and scrawny, he had a fringe
of unkempt snow-white hair and was wearing faded overalls
and long underwear that were obviously kin to the ones on
the line.

"Howdy, Orlo," Brad called.

"Come on in and set a spell, Brad. Got coffee on the
stove." The old man gave Carly a curious look, his pale
gray eyes taking a quick but unlascivious inventory of her,
apparently classifying her in some obscure way. Judging by
the way Orlo's jaw met his nose, he didn't have a tooth left
in his head.

"I think we'll pass on it, thanks," Brad answered, to
Carly's relief. "This is Carly Meadows. Carly, this is Orlo
Carney."

"Howdy."

"Hi," Carly responded, warily surveying her surroundings. Orlo's front yard was a tangle of scrap metal, old
stoves, gaping refrigerators, rusting bedsprings, and half-
dismantled appliances. Scratching and picking their way
around the junk were a handful of bedraggled chickens and

a few microcephalic guinea hens. A scrawny rooster perched imperiously on the cracked roller of a wringer washing machine, cocked a hostile eye at her, and gave vent to a creaky crowing.

"Orlo's the best trash collector in town," Brad informed her.

"Looks like he's kept most of it," Carly blurted out unthinkingly as she eyed the heaps of detritus.

To her relief, Orlo laughed instead of taking offense. "Why do you think he called me a collector?" he cackled.

"Orlo's been into recycling since before the word was invented," Brad noted.

"I'm sorry, I didn't mean to be rude," Carly apologized.

"No offense taken," Orlo assured her. "You need a pump for your washer or to water your garden, I got it. Got refrigerator shelves make great barbecue grills—after I burn the plating off 'em, that is. I can make you a trash burner out of an old washer..."

"I think she gets the idea, Orlo," Brad interrupted. "We came to check out your barn."

"Wait'll I go get the key," Orlo said. "Gettin' so's you got to keep everything locked up these days. Durn city people with their thieving city ways coming up here all the time."

Carly winced and glanced at Brad. He was whistling quietly and seemed to be enjoying himself immensely. She wondered what he was up to.

A few minutes later, Orlo was leading the way along a twisting path through the weeds and junk toward a huge, decrepit barn. After wrestling with a fistful of keys, he unfastened an ancient brass padlock that would bring a fortune in New York City. Carly wondered whether to ask about it. The door swung open on groaning hinges, revealing a gloomy, dank interior. In the shaft of light from the door, Carly could see dusty, ramshackle shelves disappearing into the cavernous distance. They were littered with tools, toasters, waffle irons, blenders, electric motors, mixers, radios, and a thousand items she couldn't identify.

"What're you looking for?" Orlo asked suspiciously.

Carly had just opened her mouth to explain when Brad jabbed her in the ribs.

"We'll know it when we find it," he answered for her.

"I trust you," Orlo told Brad. "But I ain't so sure about her," he added dubiously.

"I'll keep an eye on her," Brad told him solemnly.

"I'd come with you, but I got canning to do. I don't watch it, the durn pressure cooker's likely to blow on me. Ain't found a safety valve for it yet."

To Carly, the setup sounded positively suicidal, but she held her tongue.

"You'll need a light," Orlo announced, bending over and fiddling with something inside the door. "Here you go." He handed Brad an old automobile headlight. Wires were taped to the terminals and led to a car battery. It was the most cumbersome flashlight she'd ever seen. Also the most imaginative and the most efficient.

Carly reached for Brad's hand as he led the way into the gloom. She enjoyed the contact with him, but more, she needed the security his touch offered. She wrinkled her nose at the musty, sour odor.

"Bats," Brad explained succinctly when she asked what the stench was. Carly shivered and stared up toward the invisible rafters and beams of the old barn, sure she could hear rustlings and squeakings from overhead. She tightened her grip on Brad's hand.

The barn was a maze of shelves and junk, a hodgepodge of things apparently stored away in the order in which they'd been acquired. It was a little like an archeological dig—the farther back they went, the older the relics they found.

"See anything?" Brad asked, flashing the light around. The beam made dust motes glitter in the air.

Desperately, Carly tried to get her mind off the bats and the less than reassuring surroundings. The clutter and filth were unbelievable, but she wasn't about to complain. If ever she was going to realize her dream of turning up some long lost treasure, this was the place to do it.

"What's that straight ahead?" she asked.

"Looks like most of a 1937 Chevy," Brad decided after studying the looming hulk for a minute.

"Good Lord!" Carly put her hand on his to direct the light. The feel of his warmth and strength bolstered her courage. As she aimed the light down one narrow aisle, a gleam of gold caught her eye. She pointed and started off eagerly.

The gleam turned out to be the gilt frame around an oil painting of uncertain vintage and little value. The frame was obviously worth more than the painting. But it was something, and she set it aside and began to dig deeper into the stack of pictures leaning against a rusty milk can. A few minutes' work and she'd added six more paintings to the one she wanted, some for the frames, some for the artwork itself.

Before turning away, she gave the milk can a brief study, then decided against it. If it had had loose handles made of steel loops, she might have taken it. But with the welded handles and its condition, it wasn't worth the trouble. Standing up in the can was a bedraggled old broom made of rushes. She'd seen better imitations from Hong Kong.

After fifteen more minutes of squirming through the clutter, she had collected so much stuff they were having trouble carrying it all. Gallantly, Brad offered to carry some of her finds to the door. He set the light on a shelf and used the wires as a guide back through the maze.

Carly had never regarded herself as a coward, but after a few seconds alone in the gloom, with the stench of the bats, the creakings and rustlings she was sure weren't just her imagination, and the mysterious masses of junk looming around her, she felt terror taking root within her. She was so glad when Brad got back she reached for him with both arms.

"Well, well, well, what brought this on?" he asked, promptly taking her into his arms.

Carly's fear was supplanted by another primitive feeling as she clutched him. "This place gives me the creeps."

"Well, let's hear it for the creeps," Brad said, gently kissing the top of her head.

Carly looked up at him. His face was strangely shadowed by the light. He loomed over her, came down toward her, and her lips found his. Her fear was completely washed away by the surge of desire the kiss triggered. She was faintly aware of the light flaring around them and then winking out as Brad's arms closed around her strongly and hungrily and possessively.

In his arms there in the darkness of the reeking barn, Carly abandoned herself to her hunger. His tongue explored her teeth, her cheeks, and she sucked as if she wanted to draw him into her. She did want to draw him into her. She felt his eagerness against her belly as he pressed forward. Parting her thighs, she captured one of his powerful legs between hers. She pressed her hungry flesh against his hard muscles and squirmed to feel her breasts being flattened against him.

"Carly," Brad groaned, his hands moving down to cup her hips, to pull her against him even more, to knead her flesh lovingly, hungrily. He nibbled at her cheek, showered her face with kisses. His fingers pried their way under her belt in the back, digging for the treasure beneath her slacks.

"Oh, Brad," Carly moaned as flames raged through her. She wanted to loosen her belt, to shed her clothes, to give herself to him right then. Her fingers dug into his back and she hauled his shirt tail out so she could stroke his bare flesh, trace the line of his spine, feel the softness of his skin over the hardness of his muscles.

But when she reached for his buckle, he pulled away. "No," he groaned. "Not here, not now, not this way." His voice was ragged with desire.

Defensively, shocked at herself, Carly huddled in his arms, pressing her cheek against his chest. He stroked her back, soothing her, easing her, letting her down gently from the peak of desire she'd reached.

"Oh God, I'm sorry," Carly whispered in the darkness, glad he wasn't able to see her face, to see the shame there.

"Sorry? What for?"

Somehow she managed a nervous chuckle. Her voice echoed back weirdly from the rafters. "What must you think of me? Where's the light?" she added before he could answer.

"Down here somewhere," he answered, fumbling around at their feet. "Ah, here we are. Now where'd the damn wires go?"

In a moment he had the light on. Its glare drove back both the shadows and Carly's passion. Afraid to touch him for fear of what she might do, she kept two feet behind as he led the way to the door and daylight.

Chapter Four

IN A FEW minutes they were back out in the sunlight. Carly sucked in a deep lungful of fresh air, feeling as if she'd been freed from purgatory and heaven both. Together, she and Brad lugged her finds down to Orlo's house and set them beside a doorless refrigerator that lay on its side in front of the porch. A chicken, nesting in the freezer compartment, clucked nervously.

Carly tucked her blouse in and tried to smooth her hair back into order. She had the feeling she resembled an actress in a wild Italian movie and hoped Orlo wouldn't be able to guess what had almost happened in his barn. Brad tucked his shirt back in and shot her a look that contained lust, affection, sympathy, and amusement.

"Found something?" Orlo asked as he emerged from his abode.

There was the pungent aroma of smoke in the air, and Carly realized he must cook on a wood stove. Apparently, the pressure cooker hadn't exploded. The smell brought back a memory from her early childhood. Her great-grandmother had cooked on a wood range—a monster, black iron and white enamel, with ornate nickel handles. It had dominated a kitchen filled with delicious aromas and chintz curtains and hot pies oozing berry juices.

Desperately, Carly gathered her wits, wondering why she was thinking of such things. "These look interesting," she said cautiously, returning her attention to her job.

Orlo studied the lot cagily. His toothless mouth working, he scratched his ribs absently with one weatherbeaten hand. "Good stuff you got here," he noted at last.

Carly was acutely aware of Brad watching her. That, plus the memory of Fred's admonitions, made her uncomfortable. "How much do you want?" she asked warily.

Orlo rubbed his whiskered chin, and she had the feeling he was studying her more than he was the things she'd picked out. He did move forward to shift something, but he was looking at her rather than the painting in the ornate frame. She braced herself mentally as he stepped back.

"Eight hundred for the lot," he announced.

Carly barely managed to avoid sucking in a shocked breath and was relieved to see Brad wince noticeably. She also saw the sharp glint in Orlo's faded gray eyes as he watched her closely.

"Good stuff you got here," Orlo noted again. "That frame there's real gold. And them statues is marble all the way from Italy."

"Eight hundred," Carly repeated softly to herself as she mentally inventoried the stack of paintings, statuary, bric-a-brac, and rusty, bat-fouled implements. She thought, too, of The Gallery's financial state.

She steeled herself and mentally prayed that Brad wouldn't jostle her elbow. "Come on, Brad, let's get them back to the barn," she ordered, bending to pick up one of the statues. She sighed with relief when he reached for the paintings without a word of protest.

"What's the matter?" Orlo demanded sharply.

"Ridiculous, isn't it, Brad?" Carly asked, still praying he would go along.

"If you say so," Brad said agreeably.

"Uh—seven hundred," Orlo offered quickly.

"Don't worry, Orlo, we'll put everything back right where we found it," Carly assured him, turning toward the barn, two statues in her hands. Suddenly, she was enjoying this very much.

"Six hundred," Orlo called out, quickly tacking on another fifty when Carly hesitated.

"I think these statues came from back by that old Chevy, didn't they, Brad?" Carly asked loudly as she followed him toward the barn. She could hear Orlo behind her, scattering chickens as he tried to catch up.

"How about you make me an offer," Orlo said desperately, panting. "Come on back to the house and we can talk it over."

"Two hundred," Carly said promptly, turning around to follow Orlo back down the weedy path through the junk. "Come on, Brad."

"Two hundred!" Orlo yelped. "Five hundred...and

twenty-five," he offered when Carly put her load down.

"Back to the barn, Brad," Carly sighed wearily, picking up the statues again.

"Four seventy-five," Orlo responded quickly.

"Two fifty," Carly answered. "That painting in the gilt frame isn't worth a plugged nickel. I'm only taking it for the frame."

"Good frame," Orlo insisted. "Four hundred and fifty."

"The gilding's probably shot from acids in the dirt," Carly pointed out reasonably. "And the marble for these statues may have come from Italy, but the carving was done in a factory in New York City about fifty years ago. Three hundred." She was keeping one eye on Brad, who was standing patiently with the stack of paintings in his powerful grasp. He was watching the haggling as if it were a tennis match. She hoped that was a gleam of amusement she saw lurking behind his studiously bland expression.

"Four twenty-five," Orlo offered, giving her the feeling he was close to tears.

"Put those down a minute, Brad. Let me think." She waited.

"Four hundred," Orlo put in.

Carly didn't say anything, just began studying the array carefully. She picked up one of the statues and turned it in the sunlight, tilting it to study the bottom. Then she knelt down to inspect one of the paintings more carefully. Gently, she brushed off a little of the dirt that was caked on it.

"Four hundred it is," she announced at last, rising to her feet, wiping her hands absently on her slacks. She studied Orlo's reaction with wry amusement. The old codger was positively glowing and trying his best to conceal it. She considered telling him that no matter what he thought, he hadn't taken her—then realized it would totally spoil his day if she did. She glanced at Brad.

"If you're trying to impress me," Brad announced, "forget it."

"Why would I want to impress you?" Carly asked distractedly, her mind only half on what he'd said. "Why don't you take those to the car and get me my purse so I can give Orlo a check . . ."

"I don't take checks," Orlo announced.

"Travelers' checks?" Carly offered. "Good as cash."

"Not to me. Cash," Orlo insisted.

"I'll back her up, you old horse thief," Brad announced, returning with her purse. "You always know where to find me."

"You good for it?" Orlo asked suspiciously. "Never thought you had a pot to p . . . put a penny in."

"I think I can swing it," Brad assured him dryly.

"I've got the cash, so don't worry about it," Carly said, handing Orlo the money. She was used to doing business in cash, but hadn't planned on this big an outlay so soon.

"Don't hold with banks," Orlo grumbled, taking the bills. Wetting one grubby index finger, he counted carefully, his lips moving as he mumbled to himself. When he finished, he dug into his pocket and hauled out a rubber-banded roll of cash big enough to choke a horse. Out of the corner of her eye, Carly could see Brad gaping at the wad. Giving him a nudge, she bent to pick up a statue.

"Why in the world did you pay so much for that junk?" Brad demanded as they pulled away from Orlo's.

"And you accuse me of being a swindler," Carly retorted.

"The whole lot won't bring more than a couple of hundred. So where's your profit? To say nothing of covering your costs."

"Which only goes to show how little you know about antiques. Those buys alone'll make this whole trip worthwhile," Carly retorted. "And why the sudden change of heart? I thought I was the swindler trying to steal poor folks' priceless heirlooms."

"As for ripping off Orlo, those weren't his treasures. He'd scrounged them up from all over the county for nothing in the first place. Besides, I was having a grand old time watching you two trying to stiff each other. You know what I think?"

"What?"

"I think what happened in the barn warped your judgment," he answered wickedly.

"Oh ho ho," Carly retorted. "You think a little smooching with you in a bat-ridden barn's going to warp my judgment? If anything, the fact that I let you kiss me at all proves that my judgment was warped long ago!"

She was jammed against her seat belt when Brad slammed on the brakes, making the car slew drunkenly on the dirt road. "Oh, is that so?" he asked, his tone lightly challenging.

"What are you doing?" she asked nervously, edging away from him as he turned toward her.

"Just trying to find out if your judgment is still warped."

When he touched her, she found herself totally unable, and unwilling, to resist. Instead, she let him unfasten her seat belt so he could draw her close. His kiss started out tender, but soon was anything but. She stroked up around the back of his neck and her fingers combed into his thick, black hair as his tongue ravished her. His whiskers scraped her tender cheek, and she was aware of his heady, musky scent.

With a smothered whimper, she responded ravenously. Her breasts hurt, and when his hand inched toward one aching mound, she arched her back invitingly. His fingers slid over her throbbing flesh, and the lace of her bra made her nipple burn. He kneaded until she felt as if she were going to dissolve. Her hand slid down from his neck, down over his powerful chest, to his thigh. Seeking him, finding his power.

With a lurch and a crunch, the station wagon buried its nose in a bank of gravel and the right front wheel settled in the ditch. Carly was pitched against the steering wheel, and the horn blared. Brad muttered a curse as he tried to get the two of them untangled and regain control of the car, now that it was too late.

With a moan, Carly clamped his face between her palms, loving the sandpaper roughness of his beard. She planted a hearty kiss on his lips and tasted blood. Backing away, she touched his lip where it had been cut by her teeth when the car hit the bank. "You nut! Now whose judgment is warped?"

Forgetting the car, he looked into her eyes, and she felt as if she were going to disappear into the intense depth of his gaze. "What are you, anyway?" he asked wonderingly, warily.

"What's the matter?" she asked impishly. "Your judgment warped?"

"I think my whole mind is warped."

"Probably," she agreed, feeling ridiculously young and happy. She touched his bleeding lip again, and then lasciviously licked the blood off her finger.

"Why don't you go right to the source?" he invited.

Deliberately, battling her own desire, Carly managed to get herself untangled from him and the steering wheel. "Oh, I don't think so," she answered vaguely. "Don't you think you should try to get us out of the ditch you drove us into?" she added when he reached for her again.

"You distracted me," he pointed out, turning to study the situation.

"It wasn't my idea," she reminded him, refastening her safety belt.

"I don't think it's a real problem."

"You? Me? Us?" she asked, misunderstanding.

"The car in the ditch," he answered, shifting into reverse.

"On the other hand . . ." Carly noted when the rear wheels spun in the gravel.

"No problem," Brad said, grabing the second shift lever to put the car in four-wheel drive. With a lurch, the brawny station wagon heaved itself out of the trench. A small avalanche poured off the bank where the right fender had dug in. Thanks to the cushion of leaves and humus, no damage had been done.

"You really think that stuff you got from Orlo is worth what you paid?" Brad asked when they were back on a paved road.

"I wouldn't have paid what I did if I didn't. Those statues are good marble—maybe not the work of a great master, but definitely commercial."

"What ever happened to *ars gratia artis?*" Brad inquired wryly.

"It starved to death. Speaking of which . . ."

"How about some lunch?"

"You buying?"

"What's the matter, Orlo bankrupt you? If he did, it was your own stupid fault."

"I am a liberated woman, and I don't want to get too deeply in debt to you," she explained primly.

"I've tried flattery, I've tried bribery, and now you're denying me usury," Brad grumbled.

"If you want to try usury, I'm not going to spoil your fun."

"Will it work?" he asked hopefully, shooting her an ardent glance.

"I doubt it," she answered brightly.

"You like Mexican food?"

"I love it."

Half an hour later, they were in a booth in a cellar restaurant in Oneonta. *Piñatas* hung from the ceiling and the furniture was heavy, dark wood. They were sharing a pitcher of beer and nibbling on corn chips dipped in a tangy hot sauce. On Brad's recommendation, Carly ordered a salad in a bowl made of pastry. It was delicious. The fluted shell held a mound of lettuce, tomatoes, shredded carrots, and sliced green peppers.

She was glad Brad didn't press her about what had happened in the barn. She didn't dare try to put words to it. Besides, any words she could think of couldn't be used in mixed company. As for what was happening between them . . . well, that too was better left unanalyzed.

"So what are your plans for this afternoon?" Brad asked as they waited for the check.

"Well, first of all, I have to go to a bank so I can replenish my cash."

"So you can rip off more unsuspecting locals?"

"Unsuspecting, my foot. Orlo made out like a bandit. Did you see the gleam in his eye while he counted his profit? No, so I can pay my own way and don't have to be beholden to a monomaniacal wood-carver . . ."

"Canoe builder."

". . . wood-carver like you," Carly finished triumphantly. "Now, if you sold your carvings as well as your canoes, then you could afford to keep me in the style to which I have become accustomed. But as it is, I'll bankrupt you if I'm not careful."

"But what a way to go," Brad said, sighing theatrically.

"Poor but happy?"

"Yep. Anyway, keeping you is a style to which I would like to become accustomed," Brad observed as he paid the bill.

Carly replayed this in her mind. "Isn't that all scrambled up from what it's supposed to be?"

"I meant what I said. You ever been in a canoe?"

"Is that some kind of kinky proposition?" Carly asked as she slid out of the booth.

"It's an invitation."

"I'm supposed to be working this trip," she protested.

"Well, you could always say you were working on me, trying to change my mind."

"What makes you think I'm not? Anyway, yes, courtesy of the Girl Scouts of America, I have been in a canoe."

"So why don't you go canoeing with me this afternoon and try to change my mind?"

Carly felt delightfully wicked, like she was skipping school, and promptly agreed. "But I really do need to cash some travelers' checks."

"No problem. We'll stop by the bank in Otego," he noted as he opened the car door for her.

"Incidentally," Carly began as they headed out of town, "if anything of Orlo's turns out to be really valuable, I'll make sure he gets a fair share."

"Real altruist, aren't you?" Brad inquired skeptically.

"You sound like you don't believe me," Carly grumbled.

"Maybe I'm suspicious of your motives."

"Huh?"

Brad shrugged. "You know how I feel. Maybe that's why you're being so generous."

Carly thought about this, and the more she did so, the less she liked it. She carefully kept her temper in check. "That has got to be one of the most conceited, rude insinuations I've ever heard!"

"How so?" he asked innocently.

Her arms folded, Carly glared at him. "In the first place, it implies that I care enough about you to try to 'buy' you."

"Don't you?" he asked with wide-eyed innocence and a teasing smile.

"And in the second, it implies that I have the moral standards of a weasel," she added angrily. "Not that it's any of your business, but giving the seller a cut of any unexpected profit has always been a standard policy of mine." It was not a policy Fred approved of at all.

"You didn't answer my last question," Brad pointed out as they paused at the light by Burger King.

Carly was so irritated she ignored him. "I think you'd better get your head screwed on straight," she said tightly. "You're trying to put me in a no-win situation. If I try to haggle a price down, then I'm taking advantage of someone. If I don't, I'm only trying to impress you. If that's the way you feel about me, why do you keep seeing me?"

"Because I dig your body," Brad answered with an exaggerated leer. Then he became serious. "I'm sorry."

"For seeing me?"

"For insulting you," he said contritely. "I fully intend to keep seeing you, at every opportunity."

"Even if I resist?"

"Will you?" he asked, shooting her an appraising glance.

"I doubt it," Carly admitted with a sigh. Mulling over the conversation, she wondered just what he did see in her. If that was really the way he viewed her—as a shyster out to swindle people—how could he continue to be so ardent?

Unless, of course, he did only want her for her body. It wasn't a comforting thought. She was still worrying the problem when Brad pulled up at the small bank in the village.

"Something wrong?" he asked as she got out of the car.

"Nothing," she responded unhappily. Damn all men, anyway! She'd been honest, with herself and with him, when she'd said she wasn't likely to resist him much. Why did he have to be such a desirable hunk? And why did she have to be such a sucker for artists? Who needed all their conceits and eccentricities?

As she walked through the bank's small vestibule, Carly's eye was caught by a pair of paintings on the wall behind the tellers.

"Where'd those paintings come from?" Carly asked the teller as she bent over the checks.

"Millicent Thorpe had them in her attic. When they were decorating the bank, they advertised for something to add atmosphere and Millicent brought them over."

"I wonder if she has any more like them," Carly mused carefully. "Does she live near here?"

"Just down the block. She inherited a house full of stuff like that when her mother died."

"Really!" Carly responded, taking the cash. "Isn't that interesting. Thank you very much."

"You're welcome."

"What was all that chatter about?" Brad inquired as he held the door open.

"Those paintings are just the sort of thing I'm looking for. I was finding out if there might be some more."

"Looking for another target to rip off?" Brad asked with a smile.

"Don't you ever stop?" Carly retorted with exasperation.

"Still want to go canoeing?" Brad asked as he started the car.

"Oh. Uh, yeah, I guess so," Carly answered distractedly, her mind still on the paintings.

"Look, I don't want you doing it just to please me."

Carly frowned. "I am not doing it to please you," she said acidly.

"Oh. Why do I have the feeling I'm making a fool of myself?" Brad inquired thoughtfully.

"Because you are?" Carly asked, smiling broadly.

"It's all your fault, you know," Brad grumbled as they headed out of town.

"That you're making a fool of yourself?"

"Yes. I'm so stricken with you that I don't know what I'm doing. Or saying," he answered, flashing her a bright grin.

"Ah me, we're back to flattery," Carly sighed. "What will you try next? And why are you trying so hard? We've only known each other two days, after all. That's hardly time enough to catch a cold from each other, let alone get to know each other."

"If either of us has a cold, I'll bet the other one does, too," he chuckled.

"True," she agreed, laughing, her spirits rising steadily. "Too true."

"And as for why I'm in a hurry," he added seriously, "I don't know how long you're likely to be around, and I'm striving desperately to make a favorable impression on you in the time I have."

"Why?"

"Because I want you."

"Really? You should take an assertiveness training course. Then you wouldn't be so shy."

"How long will you be around?" he asked as they turned north off the main highway and onto his side road.

"I think I'll head back Monday," she answered, feeling her heart sink at the thought of leaving him.

"And I'm tied up tomorrow and Sunday," he said glumly. "So today is all we have."

"I'll be up this way again." She wondered why he was tied up all weekend—what he was going to be doing and with whom.

"When?"

"Just turn up some marvelous find and I'll be right here," she said lightly.

"I want you coming to see me, not some damn trinket."

"Why not both?"

"Why are you being so cagey?"

"Because I'm scared," she said candidly. "You're kind of intense."

"Part of my charm."

It was, of course. He focused his attention totally, completely. It was both flattering and exciting.

"Maybe I should ask you to pose for me," he mused.

"That is the oldest ploy in the book!"

"I know. But it works."

"Not with me."

"You won't pose for me?" he asked innocently.

Carly eyed him slyly. "Well now, that depends," she purred. "If you really mean *just* modeling, I might consider it."

"No—ah—hanky-panky?"

"Right."

"I don't think I could bear the frustration," he said, cranking the steering wheel around to aim the station wagon up his driveway.

"You're so right!"

"Now *that* is a conceited remark."

"Considering how plain you've made it how you feel about me, I don't think it is," Carly countered.

"Maybe I should just put you out of my misery and drown you," he said, sighing wearily.

"I'm a very good swimmer."

"Not with an anvil tied to your ankles," he growled.

"Well, if it makes you feel any better, I'm not at all sure I'd be able to pose for you without getting into some hanky-panky," she admitted as she got out of the car. "Which is why I have no intention of posing for you."

"No hanky-panky no matter what?" he asked, leading the way toward the barn.

"I didn't say that. But I won't let posing be used as a

ploy. When I pose, I pose. When I hanky-panky, I hanky-panky. And why are we using such a ridiculous expression, anyway?"

"Because you are a lady and I am a gentleman . . ."

"I grant only the former, not the latter," she put in quickly.

"Touché," he grunted, leading the way up a spiral stairway off the back corner of the showroom.

Carly studied the stairway curiously. It was built inside the barn's silo. She wondered what other secrets lurked in his unique house/workshop. She found out when they emerged from the silo into an enormous living area. The entire south side was windows that looked out on a spacious deck. All that broke up the gigantic room were the beams supporting the roof. In the far corner were, apparently, the bathroom and kitchen. Over them, reached by a rustic stairway, was the sleeping loft.

The furniture was natural wood, as were the walls and trim. It was all open and airy and distinctly masculine, but casually so, not overdone. She was relieved to see there were no hunting trophies.

There was, however, a superb selection of Brad's carvings, most in natural wood, but some meticulously painted to match the animals' natural colors. All were wildlife studies—woodchuck and rabbits, squirrels climbing gnarled branches, a duck with spread wings. The piece that drew Carly like a magnet was a fawn. It was so lifelike, she expected it to take flight as she approached. It stood on gangly legs, and the young deer's long, graceful neck was curved so it could lick its flank.

"Are those dollar signs I see glittering in your eyes?" Brad asked as she reached out to stroke the smooth wood.

"They are not," she said huskily. "This is too beautiful ever to put a price on."

"Thank you," he said softly, coming up behind her and putting his arms around her.

She turned in his embrace and looked up at him, marveling that this powerful man had the sensitivity to carve so beautifully.

"What's this?" he asked, picking up the elk's tooth nestling in the hollow of her throat.

"A gift from my great-grandmother."

"It looks Indian."

"It is."

"You have Indian agent ancestors that went around ripping off the poor savages?" he asked, his eyes twinkling. "Sort of a family tradition?"

"Anything but," she retorted. "We scalped agents. My great-grandmother was a full-blooded Shawnee. My relatives fought beside Tecumseh. Now, are we going canoeing today or not?"

"You wearing anything water will damage?"

"Nope," she answered, breaking out of his embrace to take the life jacket, and then inspecting the strangely shaped paddle he handed her. The blade was nearly a foot wide, and the shaft, where it joined the blade, bent at a strange angle.

"Racing paddle," he explained succinctly. "Come on, let's get out of here before I hanky-panky you in spite of my good intentions."

Back outside, he led her around to a rack of canoes in a shed.

"What other surprises do you have tucked away here? Squash courts?"

"I've always wished I had a pool table," Brad answered.

"Wishes don't count."

"If they did, we wouldn't be going canoeing right now."

"No kidding. Why don't we take one of these?" she asked, touching one of his sleek, slender racing canoes as he fiddled with a Grumman aluminum.

"Because they're kind of tippy."

Carly stiffened. "I wasn't made canoeing counselor because I went over all the time."

He studied her for a minute, as if trying to gauge how good she was. "Okay, we'll try it," he said finally. "Grab an end, squaw, and let's get this thing on the car."

As she lifted it, she almost hit herself in the jaw, the canoe was so much lighter than she expected. In a few minutes it was lashed to the station wagon's roof rack and they were headed down the driveway.

Chapter Five

FIFTEEN MINUTES LATER they were parked in a gravel lot on the banks of the Susquehanna River. Even loaded with paddles and life jackets, the canoe was easy to carry the forty feet to the steep steps down to the water. The current was slow—the bits of leaves dotting the surface were barely moving.

"Take the bow, Tecumapese," Brad ordered as he steadied the canoe against the bottom step.

"You know who she was?" Carly asked, impressed, as she stepped in carefully.

"Sister of Tecumseh, the great Shawnee war chief," he answered, joining her in the canoe. Carly reached out to grab the dock as the canoe rocked. "Here we go," he noted.

"When I say *hut*, change sides."

Totally concerned with trying to keep her balance, Carly didn't answer. Suddenly the racing canoe didn't seem like such a great idea after all. It was so low cut she felt like she was sitting in the water. Then she started paddling, and they shot away from the bank, and she lost some of her misgivings. The boat was incredibly quick and responsive.

She almost forgot to switch at Brad's first "hut." But in a few minutes she had the rhythm and they were headed upstream against the gentle current, swinging out to dodge a fallen tree lying in the water. The bent paddle seemed made to fit her. It was light and well balanced, and the wide blade provided a powerful thrust with hardly any effort at all.

"Not bad, squaw," Brad complimented her as they glided over the surface, the water barely whispering as the bow cut through it. Trees lined the banks, leaning over the water, and waterbugs danced in the shadows.

Suddenly, Carly had the feeling they were a million miles away from civilization and all its problems. No. It was more like they had dropped into a time warp and been transported back three or four hundred years. There was no sign of anything modern, only the high tree-clad banks of the river. In the distance, if she listened hard, she could occasionally hear traffic, but it was easy to ignore.

"This is glorious," Carly whispered, afraid of breaking the mystical mood.

"Look over there," Brad urged. "To the right."

At the sound of his voice, the turtle slid off a half-sunken log, and Carly could see it paddling frantically toward the safety of the bottom. A kingfisher dropped from a tree to splash in the calm water, then lifted himself back into the air, scattering spray three feet in all directions. A silvery fish flopped in his beak. Somewhere in the distance a congress of crows was debating vociferously.

At an easy pace, Brad and Carly followed the river around a curve to the left, then along a straight stretch to a meander in the opposite direction. There they came on towering concrete pylons supporting a bridge. The tranquil mood was further broken by the clatter of a car crossing overhead. But in a few minutes they'd left the modern world behind and were again alone in the wilderness.

Judging by the holes in the muddy slope, the bank of the river housed an incredible population. Something had plowed a wide track through the weeds to a field above, and a few corn stalks bobbed languidly in a backwater.

"Bank beaver," Brad explained. "Ah, there's my old buddy! Up to your left."

"What? Oh!" Carly tilted her head back and saw a feathered mass perched on an overhanging branch. Goggled yellow eyes stared down at her ferociously.

"Horned owl."

"Brad, this is incredible," Carly sighed. Forgetting where she was, she turned in her seat to look at him.

"Don't!" he warned sharply, sending the owl off its branch with his shout.

But he was too late. Carly felt the canoe tilt alarmingly from the shift in her weight, tried to correct, couldn't, and fell flat on her back into the river as they capsized. She heard Brad curse as she went under, and surfaced to hear him still swearing fluently.

"Blood of the Shawnees," he said sourly, the upward curl of his lips betraying his real view of the situation as he stood chest deep in the river.

"Now, Brad," Carly tried to soothe him, backing away as he splashed through the water toward her. She held on to the swamped canoe, trying to keep it between them.

"I'm going to get you for this," he warned. He might have if he hadn't stepped in a hole and vanished in a welter of spray, his arms flailing, his paddle smacking the water. He surfaced with an oath that echoed back off the shore and sent a heron into the air with powerful strokes of its broad wings.

"It was an accident," Carly protested as Brad shoved his hair back off his forehead.

"Boy oh boy, are you going to pay for this," he growled. There was an exciting, wicked glint in his eyes.

"Now, Brad, what are you going to do?" Carly demanded nervously, still clinging to the canoe and her paddle and trying to keep her feet up off the mucky bottom. She already had almost lost one sneaker to the ooze.

"Squaw," he growled. "Help me get this canoe over to that gravel bar. Then I'm going to paddle your bottom."

"I'm just as wet," Carly pointed out, kicking to propel the swamped canoe along.

"Irrelevant," he said, regaining his footing.

In a few minutes they had the canoe out on the sandbar. Fortunately, the sun was warm. Carly looked down at herself and realized that her sodden clothes did little to hide anything from Brad. She tried plucking at her shirt, but it just replastered itself to her breasts.

"Now I'm going to teach you a lesson," Brad announced, rubbing his hands together, grinning broadly.

"Now, Brad," Carly said, backing away, laughing.

"I'm going to get you," he insisted, starting toward her.

Desperately, Carly looked for some avenue of escape. The banks were too steep and muddy to climb, so she was trapped on the narrow spit of sand and gravel. She barely dodged his first lunge by twisting aside and splashing through the water.

Spinning, Brad advanced again, arms outstretched to block her. She feinted one way, then tried to slip past him on the other side, only to feel an arm clamp around her waist. She tried to run, to pull free, but he swung her into the air as if she were light as a feather. She was slung over his shoulder, her tangled, sodden locks trailing around her face as she kicked and squirmed, beating futilely at his powerful back.

In a moment he was sitting on a rock. Swinging her in an arc, he dropped her face down on his lap. The ease with which he subdued her she found exciting rather than frightening, and she struggled just to feel how strong he was when he held her down. She could have put up more of a fight if she hadn't been laughing so hard.

"Nononono," she pleaded through her laughter as he reached for a canoe paddle. "No, Brad, please, not that. Not a paddle. Oh you wouldn't! No! Please!"

"Oh yes I would," he said, picking one up. "Squaw must be disciplined. Squaw must learn not to tip canoe."

"You might break the paddle," she pointed out breathlessly as he raised it for the first blow.

He hesitated, then set it aside. "You're right," he agreed. "Besides, it'll be more fun this way."

Out of the corner of her eye she could see his huge hand raised over her fanny. Not about to give up, she kept right on kicking and struggling, even while she was gasping with laughter.

He delivered a half-dozen swats, each one lighter than the one before, until by the last one he was caressing her bottom with insolent intimacy. When he lifted her to sit on his lap, pulled her to him, she knew she didn't have any fight left. She met his kiss, lips hot, mobile, eager. Her tongue dueled with his. Her chest burned, and she felt as if her heart had climbed into her throat.

A powerful hand slid up and captured one of her breasts and she arched against his grip. Her nipple ached to be free of her bra, to be pressed against his palm. He cupped her hip with his other hand, then slid it over her thigh. With a whimper, Carly let her legs part, let insistent fingers press the crotch of her jeans.

She tore her mouth free and saw the hunger in his dark eyes. She couldn't hide her own desperate yearning, nor did she want to. Her hips took on a life of their own as he tantalized her through her sodden clothes. When his fingers found the buttons of her shirt, she leaned away from him,

scratching her fingertips over his hard torso, shoving his T-
shirt up to bare his chest, exposing a mat of curly black
hair.

His fingers quickly mastered the front hook of her bra,
and then claimed the peak of her breast, tormenting her
burning nipple until she gasped with pleasure. Her lips sought
his, locked on them, and her tongue plunged into his mouth,
scraping over his teeth, tasting him hungrily. His hand slid
from her breast to the buckle of her belt, and she felt him
start to loosen it. She wasn't about to stop him.

The sound from the river made them both freeze.

"Not here," he whispered hoarsely, his hands still on her
belt. He was quivering, rigid with desire.

"Oh God," Carly whimpered with relief when she realized they were still alone. A kingfisher flew off, his call
a harsh rattle. Carly sought oblivion in Brad's kiss and his
embrace.

"Oh, dear God," she whispered against his chest as he
held her, soothing her as if she were a skittish horse.

"God, how I want you," Brad announced unnecessarily,
in a tone that came from the depths of his being.

Slowly, the tremors of her desire began to die down,
until she was just snuggled comfortably against him, aware
of his power and his desire. Frustration gnawed at her, and
fear. She wanted him as badly as he wanted her. Who was
he that he could slash through all the barriers she'd built
since Jason? She shivered at her vulnerability and clung to
Brad even more tightly, seeking security in the arms of
danger.

But the mood had been broken, and the opportunity was
past, and they both knew it.

"I don't think I've punished you nearly enough," he
teased, his voice soft and rumbly in the ear she had against
his chest.

"Some punishment," she retorted softly. "If this be punishment, then let's make the most of it."

"I intend to," he promised, tipping her head so he could
look at her. His eyes were hot with desire. He brushed a
sodden tendril of auburn hair back off her face. "You didn't
get this glorious hair from your great-grandmother."

"She married an Irishman," Carly explained. Rearranging herself more comfortably on Brad's lap, she began fastening her bra.

"A Shawnee and an Irishman?" he asked wonderingly.

"The average life expectancy of a piece of crockery in their house was six weeks," Carly said, stroking Brad's cheek until he captured her hand and kissed it. "The fact that he had a weakness for strong spirits and she was a teetotaler made life even more exciting."

"They stayed married?"

"Fourteen kids' worth." She grinned. "The only thing better than the fights was the making up."

"Obviously." Brad's knowing smile warmed her to the depths of her being. "And I suppose you come from a large family, too?"

"Two older brothers and a younger sister. I'm the black sheep of the family."

"Oh? Now, why doesn't that surprise me?" he teased, surveying her as she perched in his lap, her shirt unbuttoned and open, only her filmy bra providing a pretense of modesty.

"I ran away from home—college, really," she explained. "Straight to the big city, to Sodom and Gomorrah by the sea." She pulled her shirt closed and was beginning to button it when his hand caught hers. His touch wasn't urgent or lascivious, but gentle and caring.

"So how come you're from Iowa? The Shawnees were from Ohio."

Carly held his hand against her breast, enjoying the warmth of his touch on her still damp clothes. "They settled in Iowa after Tensquatawa screwed up Tecumseh's plans to drive the whites out of Ohio."

"You know the history," Brad observed.

"The Shawnee were a great people. And my great-grandmother made sure I knew all about them."

"Did you know her well?"

"She was my idol. I was one of the middle kids, and she was the only one who seemed to have time for me. She was incredibly old and wise, and she said she'd known Blue Jacket himself, though I'm not sure she was that old." Carly held up the yellowed elk's tooth for him to see. "This belonged to Blue Jacket."

"You always wear it?" he asked, holding it gently and reverently.

"Almost."

He released it, let it nestle again at the base of her throat. "Well, you do come by your canoeing skills honestly," he noted with a chuckle.

Carly eyed the racing canoe sourly. "That thing's tricky!"

"Very. I expected us to go over within the first hundred yards."

"Really? So why'd you agree to use it?"

"I wanted to penetrate that incredible ego of yours."

"My incredible ego? Look who's talking! You've got the Mount Rushmore of egos!"

"Me? Have an ego?"

"The truth hurts, doesn't it?"

"One more crack from you . . ."

"And what?" she challenged daringly.

"And you get another dip," he threatened, scooping her up as he got to his feet.

"Don't you dare!" She wrapped her arms even tighter around his neck, enjoying his strength and power.

"You dare me?"

"Yes . . . *No I don't!*" she yelled when he swung her out over the water.

"You take it back about my ego?" He twitched, deliberately almost dropping her into the water.

"I take it back," she assured him quickly, if sullenly.

"Good girl," he said, setting her down lightly on the gravel.

"But to paraphrase Galileo, it is still there," she teased, ready to leap to safety somehow.

"Get in the canoe, squaw," Brad growled, brandishing a paddle. "And try not to tip us over again."

"What do I get if I manage not to?" she asked, helping him get the boat in the water, then stepping in carefully.

"You don't get another beating," he answered as he joined her.

"Shucks, what fun is that?" she joked, making a quick motion that tilted them dangerously, catching it before they went over.

"Hut, woman! Change sides," Brad ordered with mock ferocity.

"Aye, aye, sir!"

They resumed their journey upstream, dodging occasional snags, paddling hard against the current where the river shallowed. As she put her back into her strokes, Carly was glad for the swimming she got in down in the city. She sensed Brad's approval as she dug her blade in as a bow rudder at one point.

Another mile upstream, they came to Otego. Working past a sandbar where a small stream entered the river, they looped around a pile of rocks under a rusty iron bridge, then headed back downstream. Watching the bank, Carly was delighted by their speed and paddled harder, picking up the pace just to see how fast they could go. Brad matched her stroke for stroke. The only disappointment was how quickly it made the trip go.

Back at the landing, it was only a few minutes' work to get the canoe up on the car rack. Her feet were still squishing in her sneakers, but the warm summer sun and air had reduced the sogginess of her clothes to dampness.

"That was great," she said happily, feeling free and clean and revitalized after the burst of exercise. She'd forgotten how much she enjoyed canoeing.

"You ought to be here in the spring for the races."

"Races?" she asked, intrigued.

"The General Clinton Canoe Regatta. Three solid days of races. The big one is seventy miles, from Cooperstown to Bainbridge, Brad explained as he started the car.

"How many days does that take?"

He laughed. "One."

"Seventy miles? In one day?" Carly remembered the day trip she'd taken as a Girl Scout. It had been less than ten miles, and she'd been exhausted.

"Longest one-day flat-water race in the world. Takes eight hours for the pros, up to twelve to fourteen for the amateurs."

"You've been in it?"

"Of course. How do you think I advertise those?" He gestured at the ceiling with a jerk of his thumb. He looked over at her as they paused for traffic at Route 7. "Want to try it next spring?"

"You need a partner?" she asked, excited and intimidated and flattered that he'd ask her.

"My last one got transferred by his company. They allow women and mixed teams."

"Well, I should hope so!"

"Huh. Liberated squaw, aren't you," Brad observed, turning left toward his home without asking.

"Never said I wasn't," she reminded him.

"Going to have to do something about that, too," he threatened.

"Ho ho," she retorted. "You talk as if you expect to see a lot of me."

"Oh, I do," he assured her.

"Don't I have anything to say about it?"

"I don't hear you protesting too much."

"I'm going back to the city Monday."

"You don't belong in the city. And anyway, you're not the type to give up. I expect you'll be around for a while, trying to get your hands on my carvings. And if you're going to race with me next spring, we'll have to get in a lot of training time."

Carly felt she should argue with at least some of his assumptions, but couldn't for some reason. Instead, she fastened on the last thing he'd said. "Did you really mean it when you asked me to paddle with you?"

"I did. Think you can handle the stern?"

"Of course. But..."

"Trust me. It's best to have the strongest paddler in the bow."

"Why? I learned the best paddler should be in the stern."

"They should, on lakes. River canoeing is totally different."

"Oh."

As she helped him unload the canoe and put the paddles and life jackets away, the tension kept building. Both of them knew what was coming. She wasn't sure how she was going to handle it.

When he did ask her to stay rather than go back to her motel, her wariness burst forth with a vengeance. The scars from Jason were still too tender. His kisses and caresses had burned, too.

"I think I'd better get back to my room. Dry clothes and all that," she explained lamely.

"I have a dryer," Brad told her, taking her firmly by the shoulders.

She looked up into his eyes, armoring herself against them as she did. Oh, how she wanted to accept. But the alarm bells were jangling everywhere, the reasons piling up. She'd learned to enjoy her independence. And he was another damn artist! She'd only known him two days! She might be mad, but she wasn't that mad!

"Maybe some other time," she managed to answer.

"Supper tonight?" he asked. "Here?"

"Can I trust you?" she asked, smiling.

"Probably not."

Carly laughed and freed herself from his grasp. "If you'd answered any other way, I'd know I couldn't. Okay, supper here. I'll keep my back to the wall at all times." She realized she didn't want to leave him, even for a moment. Oh Lord, what had she gotten herself into?

"Now, about those wet clothes of yours . . ."

"Is that a ploy to get me out of them?" she asked impishly.

"It sure is, before you catch your death of cold," he retorted. "There's a robe in the bathroom you can wear. I'll toss your stuff in the dryer and it'll be ready if you want it."

"When I want it," she corrected firmly over her shoulder.

"Should be an interesting evening," he called as she closed the door. "Just leave your stuff on the floor, and I'll get it after I change."

In a few minutes she was swaddled in his robe. Engulfed in it was more like it, she thought as she rolled up the sleeves. She emerged from the bathroom just as he came down from the sleeping loft, his own damp clothes in his huge fist.

"Drinks are out on the deck," he announced. "I'll be right with you."

Like almost everything in the house, his deck was natural wood. The only concession he had made to other materials were some aluminum and plastic lawn chairs and chaises. Flames already danced in a barbecue grill. An open bottle of wine was set out on a tray in an ice bucket, beside glasses.

After helping herself, she strolled over to the railing.

The land dropped away to the south, presenting a magnificent vista of rolling hills clothed with trees and pastures. The warm breeze in her face brought with it the scent of blackberries ripening in the sun. Somewhere below was the gurgle of a stream.

Brad had done little to tame the land. Brush grew to the edge of a small unkempt lawn. A rutted track led off to the right, down into the small valley, then up the opposite slope to disappear into the woods. She wondered if that was where he went to get the wood for his carvings.

"Enjoying the view?" he asked, emerging from the house, balancing a tray loaded with steaks and potatoes and foil.

"It's lovely. Can I do anything to help?"

"Thanks, but it's all under control," he assured her, deftly wrapping the potatoes in foil and putting them on the grill.

Settling in one of the chairs, Carly was suddenly very aware of just how little she had on under the robe. Glad it was voluminous, she folded her legs under her and carefully tucked it around her thighs, then settled back and watched Brad puttering at the grill. He had changed to cutoffs and a sweatshirt that had been relieved of its sleeves. Judging by the looks of it, he'd used a hunting knife to do the tailoring. His bare feet were set wide apart, both legs straight. They were strong and well shaped, as tanned as his arms.

"Should I be more formal?" he asked when he caught her staring.

"Oh no, I'm sorry," she apologized. "You look great."

"I look like a refugee from the Salvation Army bin," he countered. "But I'm comfortable, and you're not exactly overdressed."

"You do look great," she insisted.

"So do you."

"If I don't get my hair combed out, I'll look a fright," she protested.

"Where's your comb?"

"My brush is in my purse."

"So what are your plans for the weekend?" he asked after returning with her chic leather bag.

"I thought you were going to be out of town," she said warily, trying not to let her disappointment show in her voice.

"I am, dammit. I was just wondering."

"Oh. Well, there's an auction Saturday. Thought I'd give it a try. There might be something."

"Good luck. You'll need it around here."

"Why?"

"We have some of the cagiest auctioneers and auction goers I've ever seen."

"Do you go to many auctions?"

"Not since I bought a pool cue at one."

"But you don't own a pool table."

"No. That's why I don't go to auctions anymore," he said ruefully.

"It's easy to get carried away. Besides the auction, I have a couple of other places I'd like to check out." She was thinking of Millicent Thorpe, wondering if that would pan out.

"Anyone I know?"

"Well, there's a nut who builds canoes and also does really great wood carvings of animals," she drawled to deflect him. "But he refuses to acknowledge how much better it would be to concentrate on carvings rather than canoes."

"Sounds like a tough case," Brad observed.

"The toughest," she agreed.

"Maybe you should try seducing him."

Carly laughed. "Do you think it would work?"

"Always worth a try, wouldn't you say?"

"I'll think about it."

"You do that. Excuse me while I turn the potatoes. You want some salad?"

"Garden fresh?"

"Well, what the deer didn't get will go into it," he answered as he worked at the grill.

"Do you hunt?"

"Are you kidding? All deer have to do is take one look at me with those big, soft brown eyes of theirs and I'm helpless."

"Gee, will it work if I try it?" Carly asked, wide-eyed.

"It would if your eyes weren't so passionate," he countered.

"My eyes aren't passionate."

"Have you ever looked at them when you're feeling amorous?"

"Not likely. Where are you going?"

"Salad."

"Let me do it," she offered, glad to escape the conversational trend.

As they ate, Carly found herself opening up to Brad in ways she never had with anyone else. He drew her out about her family, inquiring further about how she'd felt ignored as one of the middle children. Kathy had been the baby of the family, she elucidated, and Jerrold had been the eldest son. Mark was the successful athlete. No one but Great-grandmother had bothered with difficult, sensitive, pensive Carly.

Brad managed, too, to draw her out about Jason, helped her see him as he really was—neither better nor worse. She realized at last that Jason probably hadn't much ability as an artist. He might scrape along with a few sales at the biannual Greenwich Village Art Show, but he'd never advance beyond that. He'd probably be able to hang on as a teacher, but he lacked the self-discipline necessary to succeed at much of anything. And to succeed at art takes more self-discipline than most things do.

Jason, Carly understood finally, loved the mystical aura conferred on him when he claimed to be an artist. It gave him a license to be unconventional, a nonconformist, a rebel. It excused his drinking, his pot smoking, his wenching, and his chronic underemployment. Carly felt badly for his gullible students—she had been one herself—but admitted, when Brad pressed her on it, that there was nothing she could do about it.

Inevitably, Carly compared Jason with Brad and found Jason wanting in every way. Brad didn't smoke at all and drank lightly. He dressed casually, but with none of Jason's flamboyant shabbiness. If Brad was a nonconformist, it wasn't deliberate, it was how he naturally was. He pursued his own goals with single-minded determination and never gave a thought to his image or what people thought of him.

Carly wondered if she was one of Brad's goals. Being with him was a little like being the target of a cannon at point-blank range. It was incredibly impressive, very flattering, to be the recipient of so much attention, and distinctly intimidating.

And all the while they were talking, again and again she

was drawn to the fawn on the coffee table. She couldn't keep from stroking it with loving fingers, caressing its cool, smooth curves.

The evening passed too quickly. He was attentive and understanding, but not demanding. After supper she sat with her legs curled under her in a comfortable chair, ignoring the invitation of his arm along the back of the sofa. When she finally forced herself to leave him to get dressed, he made his disappointment obvious, but didn't press her.

They drove back to her car, still waiting patiently in Otego, silently sharing each other's company, and frustration. Carly knew what she wanted to do, knew what he wanted to do. And they both knew that it wasn't going to happen. She wasn't ready yet, and as if by unspoken agreement, she knew that Brad would never press her before she was.

He helped her transfer the stuff she'd gotten at Orlo's to her car. The visit to the bat-infested barn seemed like centuries ago, so much had happened since. The night was alive with the sound of crickets, but otherwise the village was quiet. The streetlights created glowing pools along the sidewalk.

Carly got carefully into her car and rolled down the window. She was frankly afraid of what she might do if she let herself get trapped in one of his steaming body-to-body embraces.

"I'll see you," he said softly.

"Is that a threat or a promise?" she asked, trying to be humorous in an effort to hide her real emotions. She felt like she was dying.

"I'll see you," he assured her. "And that's a promise. Besides, we've got a canoe race in May."

"When exactly in May?" she asked, looking up at him as he loomed over her, his elbows resting on the roof of the car.

"Memorial Day."

"I'll have to check my calendar."

"You do that." Suddenly, he leaned in the window, trapping her head with one hand. His kiss was demanding, thorough, and left her breathless and aching for more. "Drive carefully."

As she watched him walk away, she put a wondering

finger to her lips. He moved lightly, gracefully, and totally confidently. His walk said he knew she'd be back. Her heart thumped its agreement, while her brain screamed useless warnings.

Chapter Six

THE FOUR-HOUR DRIVE back through the Catskills on Monday gave Carly more time to think about Brad Weston than she wanted. The afternoon sun was behind her, throwing the folds of the mountains into shadows. She'd put off leaving Otego for as long as she could, hoping against hope that Brad would come looking for her when he got back from wherever it was he'd been.

Friday night's dinner with him stood out in her mind more because of his attentiveness than either the food, which had been delicious, or the magnificent setting. He was incredibly intense. Nothing escaped those dark eyes of his, nor did the slightest nuance of her words pass him by. It was almost as if he could read her mind.

As a result, his absence had made the weekend achingly empty in spite of all she'd gotten done.

He had been right about the auction. The auctioneer had been skilled, and the crowd willing. Time and again, Carly had bid on items, then dropped out when the price went too high. If other people wanted to pay that much, let them. Maybe they didn't have a profit margin to consider. Anyway, she was not about to get suckered into a bidding war. It was easy to get carried away in a competitive situation. She was always careful to decide ahead and then stick to a fixed limit on how high she would bid.

Resting on the back seat of the car were three early American landscapes out of Millicent Thorpe's attic. They weren't Weston carvings, but they were darn good, distinctly salable, and sure profit makers.

Millicent Thorpe had turned out to be tall, long-faced, and handsome, rather than beautiful, with two toddlers clinging to her faded jeans. There had been no sign of a

Mr. Thorpe. Subsequently, Millicent had explained she was a widow, on her own and struggling.

The house wasn't as well cared for as the ones on Main Street, but it was definitely big. When the bank teller had said there was a house full of stuff, she hadn't been exaggerating. There had to be at least a half-century's accumulation. The attic had borne a distinct resemblance to Orlo's barn, right down to the bats. Only the '37 Chevy was missing.

Carly and Millicent had spent hours rummaging through the attic while the children rocked happily on an old hobby horse that had been way back under the eaves. If she'd had more money, Carly could have filled her car. She had gotten Millicent to promise she'd call Carly collect and check with her before selling anything else.

All the time she'd been at Millicent's, Carly had had the feeling Brad was peering over her shoulder. She couldn't understand how he had burned himself into her soul so deeply in only two days.

Usually, the view of the city as she crossed the George Washington Bridge gave her a thrill, reminding her of the first time she'd seen the panorama of towering buildings as her bus from Iowa had headed down the ramp to the Lincoln Tunnel. Ever since, whenever she saw the New York skyline, she got a possessive feeling, as if it were all there just for her. Today it was as impressive as ever, but it looked gray, confining, claustrophobic.

She tried to blame her feeling on the traffic, but wasn't able to. It was late afternoon, and most of the jam was headed out of town. The pollution was no worse than usual, either. Better than average, in fact.

The problem, she told herself, is not in the city but in yourself. She had the feeling she was losing something that had been very precious to her.

She chose Riverside Drive instead of her usual route down the Henry Hudson Parkway. She was willing to put up with its narrowness and traffic lights in order to get a view of Riverside Park. She felt as if she were getting one last glimpse of freedom before being sent to jail. She gave the grass and trees a final wistful look before she turned east toward Columbus Avenue.

Parking in front of The Gallery was hopeless, as always. It was a continuing mystery to her who owned the cars that lined the streets. Forced to double park, she set the emergency flashers, slid across the front seat, and scrambled out.

"You get the trunk," she ordered Fred, throwing him the keys while she reached into the back seat for Millicent's paintings.

"What is this stuff?" Fred asked rudely as he unloaded what she'd gotten from Orlo's bat-ridden barn.

"Let's not try to inventory it now. I've got to get the car back before six or they'll charge us for another day."

"But . . ."

"I'll be back in about half an hour," she called as she slipped behind the wheel. She was in such a hurry to get away, she almost put herself under the wheels of a bus. Then she cut off a taxi at 72nd Street. Wincing at the epithet she got from the cabbie, she decided she'd better forget everything else until she got the car back safely.

By the time she walked through The Gallery's door, she felt totally drained. She also felt as if she'd been away for months, rather than days, and glanced around, taking a mental inventory to see if anything had sold. The Gallery looked as neat and dignified as ever.

The paintings hanging on the pale gray walls and the bric-a-brac and statuary in the cases and on the shelves glowed under the careful lighting. One thing she had to say for Fred—he did know how to display things to their best advantage. Looking lean and elegant in his trim three-piece gray suit, as if he were on display too, he was fingering his chin as he studied her acquisitions.

"Anything from Brad Weston?" he asked without preamble.

Carly sighed. "I told you I wasn't going to get anywhere with him." She wished she could lie, tell Fred that Brad's carvings weren't as good as they were. She couldn't do it, though. She thought of Brad's carvings of the fox and the fawn and even his mailbox post, and her longing to be away from here, to be back up in Otego, grew noticeably stronger.

Carly studied her partner, taking in his carefully fluffed light brown hair. The gold frames of his glasses caught the artful gallery lighting. He did look the part of a prosperous dealer, she reflected sourly. And he did know how to lay out The Gallery to create a feeling of class—which was one of the things that separated it from other secondhand shops.

"Did you try?" he asked suspiciously.

"I did everything but sleep with him," she said without thinking.

"Five days up there in a motel, and this is all you have to show for it?" Fred persisted with a wave of one well-manicured hand.

"You're looking at it," she said wearily. Dealing with Fred had never seemed so futile and frustrating as it did now.

"It's junk!"

"It may not be great art, but it'll sell. I know what I'm doing!"

"Where did you dig up these amateur dabblings?" he asked, gesturing with the toe of his Gucci loafer. She didn't recall the shoes and wondered if he'd gone on a shopping spree. Typical. The Gallery was tottering on the brink, and he'd spend a hundred dollars on a pair of shoes. Brad's sneakers looked better and better.

"They'll sell," she insisted. If they weren't old masters, landscapes were anathema to Fred. "They're good, and you know it. Okay, so they're the kind of thing someone looking for something green to fill the space over his sofa will buy. What does that matter?" Gad! Did everything have to remind her of Brad? She recalled him using those very words in one of their arguments.

"What kind of a deal did you make?" Fred demanded. When she told him, he shot her a baleful glare. "And what about this stuff?" he asked, indicating the objects from Orlo's. "And what is that gunk all over that statue?"

"Bat droppings," Carly informed him with relish. She was rewarded with a gratifying gasp of revulsion. "I found those, with Brad Weston's help, in an old geezer's barn. He started out asking eight hundred. I got him down to half that."

"He should have paid you to take them," Fred said, sniffing disdainfully.

"Most of it's in the twenty- to fifty-dollar range. But the

statues are good, even though there aren't any signatures."

"Imitation Rodin," Fred observed. *Imitation* was one of his classic put-downs when he was discussing one of her purchases. Why was it whenever he bought something it was almost certainly an original?

"Obviously," Carly said wearily. "But Rodins, imitation or genuine, always sell."

"What about your motel bill?" Fred asked as she headed for the door. "I suppose you stayed at the best place in town?"

"I stayed at the only place in town," she snapped. "Now, good night. I'm tired. I'll see you tomorrow."

She fled before he could pry any deeper. Why hadn't she taken as much care and time in picking her business partner as she would in picking a mate? Then she thought of Jason and winced. She sure hadn't taken enough time there. Had she learned anything? Was she making another mistake? Then she resolutely set all thoughts of Brad aside to consider a more immediate problem. Was it her imagination, or was Fred getting harder and harder to deal with?

A week after her return from Otego, Carly was still pondering the same question. Maybe it was just that her patience with Fred was exhausted. It seemed that whenever she wanted to spend money it was "frivolous" or "too expensive" or "too risky." But if he wanted to, he could always come up with some reason.

Mercifully, her trip upstate had turned out to be more successful than even she had hoped. Millicent's landscapes had looked great on the wall. A decorator working on an apartment near Lincoln Center had come in to look at something else and had bought two of them.

A few of the items from Orlo's cache had already sold, right in the range she'd predicted. The statues had been snapped up by a little old lady whose cheeks had turned pink as she'd lifted the more daringly undraped of them to study it surreptitiously. One oil painting in a rosewood frame had been cleaned up nicely and would command a decent price from someone in search of a still life for the dining room.

So why, Carly asked herself, didn't she feel better about

everything? She sat back from brushing the crud out of the
crevices in the ornate gilt frame from Orlo's. She hadn't
even bothered to remove the worthless canvas from it. Wearily, she pushed a lock of hair back off of her face.

Telling herself that the problem was Fred didn't work.
Fred had always been difficult. It wasn't anything new. He
had delusions of grandeur, among other problems. Carly
attributed them to his Yale degree going to his head. To
him, The Gallery was an art gallery rather than a glorified
secondhand shop. She'd discovered his willingness to skate
on the fringes of outright fraud in some of his dealings the
first month they'd been open. Well, maybe it wasn't fraud,
but he did tend to view their stock in an extremely optimistic
light and peddle it that way.

Carly didn't like it, but had long ago wearied of making
an issue of it. She conducted her business her way, and
Fred did his, his. Neither of them was going to change. And
in spite of Fred, she enjoyed the work.

So why, Carly asked herself again, did she feel so gray?
No, not just gray. She felt black. Bending over her work,
she blew the loosened dirt out of the crack, brushed some
more, and blew again. The cleaned gilding glowed richly.

Maybe, she mused, it was because she'd failed to con-
vince Brad about his carvings.

Then she shook her head, making her thick locks brush
her shoulders, and finally got a grip on herself and forced
herself to admit the real reason for her gloom.

Brad Weston. Not his work, not his carvings, but the
man himself. Brad Weston was the source of her misery.
She had no idea if she would ever see him again. Her future
lay stretched out ahead of her, blank and gray and empty.

There had been all sorts of hints that she'd see him again.
But she couldn't help thinking they were exactly the kind
of things people say after meeting at a party—meant at the
time but never followed up on. "Oh, you must drop by
sometime." "Give me a call and we'll get together for lunch."
"I'll see you around."

Besides, there was no "around" that she and Brad shared.
Brad's "around" was two hundred miles away. And try as
she would, she couldn't take seriously his invitation to paddle in the race with him. He was a pro and she'd never

paddled more than ten miles in one day in her life—that on an outing at her camp, and said outing had been more years ago than she cared to admit.

The electric eye guarding the door chimed softly, alerting Carly to a customer. Dusting off her hands, she shed her work apron before she emerged from the back room. Fred was a real bug for appearances, and Carly did her best to meet his standards without breaking her budget. The conservative dark gray slacks she was wearing were from the bargain basement at Macy's. Her soft, ruffled blouse was a shade of peach that made her skin glow and her already dark brown eyes look black.

"Oh hi, Ricardo," she greeted the mailman as he set down a box two feet high and half again as long.

"Express Mail," he announced in his charmingly accented English. "Twenty-four hours, or your *dinero* cheerfully refunded."

"Did you make it?"

"The San Juan Flash always makes it," he retorted with pride, his gold tooth gleaming. "Sign here."

Carly signed where indicated. Probably something Fred had ordered, though why it would come Express Mail was a mystery. She didn't look at the return address until after Ricardo had stripped off his receipt and she'd picked up the box and started back to the workroom. When she did look, she almost dropped the parcel.

"Brad Weston, R.D. 1, Otego," she read softly. Instantly, she was back on his country road, looking up his rutted driveway to where he lounged in his doorway, arms folded.

She sank down, adjusting quickly when she almost missed the stool. Her hands shaking, she rested the package on her knees. It was addressed to her. It was tall enough and long enough and deep enough. She had the feeling she could see right through the heavy brown paper.

Grabbing a pair of scissors, she hacked through the tough packing tape. Then she tore the paper off frantically. The box opened like the petals of a flower when she slit all the tape. Wads of newspaper avalanched around her feet, revealing the treasure.

Blinking back tears of joy, Carly gently touched the carved neck of the fawn, traced the shell-like thinness of one ear with her fingers. She wondered again how Brad could capture the vitality of an animal in wood.

For a long time all she could do was sit there, while wild feelings chased through her. Oh Lordy, Lordy, Lordy, how could she feel so much? How could she feel so much and still manage to breathe?

Feeling as if she were in a dream, she reached for the card that was tucked carefully into the curve of the fawn's neck. Her fingers shaking, she tore the envelope open. His handwriting was firm, carefully formed, yet impatient and bold. It was black slashes on snowy white paper, and it took her a moment to translate the marks into letters, the letters into words, the words into thoughts.

My dearest Carly, I know you want this. Watch over him carefully, he's barely weaned. I will see you again . . . soon.

Twenty minutes later, she was still sitting there admiring the carving. She was studying every curl of the grain, every chisel mark, every line of muscle and sinew and bone that Brad had brought out of the wood. She felt as if she were getting to know Brad just by studying his work.

"My dearest Carly," she whispered to herself, glancing at the note again. She wondered if the salutation meant as much to him as it did to her.

Fred's sudden entrance was jarring. He began by berating her for not responding to the bell when he'd come in, and it gave her a second to focus her attention on him and gather her scattered wits.

"Where did that come from?" he demanded, interrupting himself.

"It's from Brad Weston," Carly answered without thinking.

"So that's a Weston," Fred observed wonderingly. "It's everything you said his work was. More!" He reached out to touch it.

"It's mine!" Carly said sharply, defensively, encircling it protectively with her arms.

"What?" Fred blinked at her through his gold-rimmed glasses, and Carly noticed suddenly how pale and pasty he looked.

Desperately, she straightened up, took a deep breath, and tried to get a grip on herself. "It just came Express Mail, addressed to me. It's a gift. To me."

"Oh come on now, you can't be serious," Fred protested anxiously. "Let me see the card."

Carly snatched it away from him and almost tucked it inside her bra in an effort to keep it safe. "No. It's a personal note and doesn't have anything to do with The Gallery."

"You've got to be kidding!" His eyes kept returning to the fawn. "You're not going to keep that to yourself, are you?"

Carly touched the statue tenderly, turning it a fraction. "I most certainly am."

Fred took a deep breath, then began pacing the workroom.

"So, was there anything good at the auction?" she asked, trying to change the subject. Fred was still staring at the fawn hungrily.

"You wouldn't believe what some people are willing to pay for *kitsch*," he observed sourly. "I thought we were partners."

"What does that have to do with the auction?" Carly asked, dazed.

"Nothing," Fred snapped, exasperated. "I'm talking about that." He gestured toward the statue with both hands, and Carly fought the urge to snatch it away to safety.

"You can't keep that for yourself! Think of the price it would bring!"

Carly was horrified. "Fred, you can't be serious!"

"I most certainly am. We're running a business here, as I seem to constantly need to remind you. We're here to make a profit. We're in this together, share and share alike. And The Gallery paid your expenses on that little jaunt."

Carly was too startled to be angry. She couldn't believe her ears. "You're out of your mind!"

"No I'm not," Fred retorted huffily. "If anyone is out of their—his—her mind, it's you."

"Oh damn the grammar, you overeducated twit!" Carly exploded. "That statue is a *gift*! A *personal gift*. From the artist. To me! It's MINE!"

"Still a sucker for artists, aren't you?" Fred asked snidely. Not for the first time, Carly wished she'd never told him about Jason.

She took a deep breath, reining in the Irish and the Shawnee in her. She felt very close to scalping her partner.

"What is between me and Brad Weston is none of your damn business," she pointed out with an icy calm that should have warned him.

"What did you do? Pose for him in the nude?" Fred prodded nastily. "That would explain how you spent so much time up there and came back with so little. In terms of art works, that is. I hope you at least took precautions."

It was the last straw. All the frustrations of dealing with Fred suddenly boiled over and a red haze filled her vision. Without even thinking about it, she picked up the frame she'd been cleaning. Totally oblivious of the fact it still had a painting in it, she brought it down on her partner's head. The aged canvas burst over his carefully tended hair. Picking up Brad's carving, scattering wrappings behind her, Carly stormed through the door into the showroom. She pushed past a dignified, startled couple without a word, charged out the door, and ran down the street to her apartment.

When she thought about it later, remembered how Fred had looked, she rocked back on her sofa and laughed until the tears streamed down her cheeks. The frame had been jammed down around his shoulders, the torn canvas forming a ludicrous collar around his neck. His glasses had been knocked half off, and dust and fragments of paint and bat droppings had covered his head and shoulders like multi-colored dandruff. The whole thing was positively cathartic. She hadn't laughed so hard since she'd returned from Otego.

She thought of how much Brad would have appreciated the scene. Anyone who ran dealers off with clay missiles would love seeing one of them so suitably framed.

Then Carly looked at the carving resting on—over-whelming—her shabby little coffee table and felt herself melting.

Oh, Brad, what are you trying to do to me? After Jason, she'd managed to construct a nice, safe, conservative life. She had her apartment, with its carefully assembled treasures. Her spider plant was thriving, hanging in the center of the big window looking out on West 71st Street. She had all of New York City to draw on, its museums and galleries and plays and movies and concerts. She had it all together.

And Brad Weston was threatening to bring it all tumbling down around her ears. Like the painting she had ringered around Fred, she realized, smiling. She'd had no idea how much she wanted to shatter his Ivy League pomposity. The blatant greed with which he'd regarded her fawn had been the last straw.

She thought of his crack about The Gallery paying for her trip and felt her fury rising again. He'd stood there and had the gall to say that? She should have brained him with a statue instead of a painting.

She'd thought better of him. She still couldn't believe he'd tried to get her to part with the carving. All right, so they were running a business. That didn't give him the right to lay claim to a personal gift. Unable to resist, she reached out and stroked the cool wood. It felt as if Brad had oiled it lightly.

There was the faintest scent of lemon oil, and that brought back vivid memories of his miraculous house. She suddenly realized that the smell had been with her all the time she'd been there but that she hadn't consciously noticed it. Now she could almost see Brad in his cut-off jeans and hacked-off sweatshirt, and she felt as if her insides were being slowly compressed. She wondered what Brad was doing at the moment and visualized him in his spacious, rustic living room, surrounded by his carvings.

Getting to her feet, Carly poured herself a glass of wine and silently toasted Brad's creation. She thought the fawn had a gleam of amusement in his carved eye. He looked like he was laughing about the scene with Fred.

Probably, what had happened would mean the end of their partnership. Carly felt a twinge of concern at the realization. It had been a fairly comfortable arrangement, in its way. Fred had handled his end of it, and she hers. And there hadn't been any emotional entanglements. From the first there had never been any sexual attraction between them. She had wondered for a while if he was gay.

The shriek from the downstairs buzzer jarred her out of her silent, loving study of the carving. Reluctantly, she got up and pressed the intercom button.

"It's Fred," he announced, his voice so tinny she couldn't gauge his mood. She buzzed him in and used the time it took him to climb the three flights of stairs to brace herself for the encounter.

She admitted him, warily, and watched his eyes go to the statue the moment he was through the door. But after that one hungry glance, he pointedly avoided looking at it again. She was relieved to see his glasses were straight and unbroken. He'd brushed off the paint and crud and combed his hair. He looked as civilized as ever, in fact.

"I came to apologize," he began, and she felt a wave of relief. "I was out of line to suggest there was anything improper between you and Mr. Weston."

"Whether there is or there isn't is none of your business. And I don't appreciate your throwing Jason up in my face."

"That was inexcusable on my part," he acknowledged sullenly.

"I'm glad you realize that." When the silence stretched on and on, she decided he was waiting for her to say something more. "And I'm sorry I hit you with the painting."

"It's a total loss."

"It wasn't worth much. Sometimes I'm not as civilized as I should be."

"About the carving . . ." he began.

"The carving is not a matter for debate," she interrupted coldly. She'd been watching the way he'd finally begun surreptitiously studying it.

"No, no, no, I see your point," he assured her quickly. "I was just caught off guard, and my—well, I spoke hastily."

Biting back a crack about his greed, Carly mumbled something about understanding.

"Would you—ah—be willing to display it at The Gallery?" he asked hesitantly. "We'd mark it *Not For Sale,* of course. It would at least bring in some customers. It's an exquisite work, really wonderful. One of his best, I imagine."

Carly mulled over Fred's suggestion—which did have merit. They needed something to attract people to The Gallery. "I'll think about it," she replied at last.

For a moment she was afraid he was going to give her an argument. Then he gave a resigned sigh and relaxed. "No hard feelings?"

Deciding it was safe to haul out the peace pipe, Carly nodded and offered him a drink. The partnership was, apparently, still intact. She wasn't sure whether she was relieved or not.

"You do seem to have had an effect on Mr. Weston," Fred noted.

"Apparently," Carly agreed, carefully keeping her tone as level as she could.

"Now, don't misunderstand me," Fred began warily, "but, don't you think there's a chance you could get him to change his mind?"

Carly thought for a moment. She didn't think about Fred's question, exactly, because she knew how much chance there was of changing Brad's mind. Rather, she tried to come up with an answer Fred could understand and accept.

"His mind seems made up," she said after a short silence.

"Would you be willing to keep trying?"

Would I? Carly asked herself. Does the sun rise in the east? "I might," she said cautiously.

"I'll have to review the budget," Fred mused. "But if the last Thorpe item does as well as the other two, I believe we could finance another trip up to Otego. *If* you think you could definitely bring back some more things from her collection. You did say there's more there? And that she's promised everything to us? Anyway, perhaps you could confer with Mr. Weston again." He cleared his throat.

Carly managed, somehow, to keep herself on a tight rein. Her heart was soaring, and she was ready to leave right then. "I have plenty here to keep me busy for a while." Dammit, she couldn't let Brad know how he affected her. And she couldn't get involved with him. It would work havoc with her carefully plotted life. And besides, what if she was totally misreading his note and gift?

"Probably wise," Fred agreed suavely. "We'll table that for a while and see how well the last Thorpe does. Meanwhile, why don't you call her and make sure she isn't selling stuff behind our backs."

"I would like to talk with her," Carly answered vaguely, sure Millicent would never do such a thing after promising Carly she'd check with her before selling anything else. Carly had the feeling that she and Fred were waltzing warily around each other. Their relationship had never been intimate, but a new note of caution had been introduced by the afternoon's explosion.

After he left, Carly eyed the statue. She wondered if Brad had any idea of the consternation he had caused at

The Gallery. And she wondered how long she'd be able to hold off going to him.

"Damn all artists," she growled, lifting her glass in a toast in the direction of the fawn, then downing the last of her wine.

Chapter Seven

AFTER THE WAY the steep ramp to the upper level of the George Washington Bridge had nearly done in the rental car—this time a Valiant—Carly wondered if the poor thing would survive the long, hilly drive to Otego. She hoped she wouldn't have to open the hood—she was afraid if she did she'd find a pair of malnourished chipmunks as a power source. She changed lanes cautiously so she'd be able to make the Palisades Parkway exit.

At least the windshield wipers worked, vigorously sweeping aside the misty rain. Heavy clouds hung like a pall over the city. She had the vague feeling that she was driving out from under a shadow all her own.

There wasn't anything definite she could put her finger on. Fred had been on better behavior than usual. She'd even entrusted her precious fawn, since christened Pan, to Fred's care at The Gallery. After a burglary in her apartment building, she'd come to the conclusion Pan was safer with Fred and the shop's burglar alarms and locked gates than in her apartment while she was out of town.

As the tires hissed on the wet pavement, Carly managed to find WQXR on the car radio. Humming along with Beethoven's *Pastorale* symphony, she left New York behind. She'd been on the phone to Millicent, and both of them were looking forward to getting together again, and not just to explore the attic. The beginnings of a potential friendship had sprouted between them.

Brad, too, was expecting her. When her phone bill arrived, she was going to be bankrupted, but she didn't care. She didn't remember what she and Brad had talked about, what they'd said. All she remembered was that she had clung to the phone and the sound of his voice as if they made a lifeline. She hadn't talked that long on the phone since high school. He had invited her to stay with him, but

she'd sidestepped that, much as she wanted to take him up
on it.

As she swung onto the New York State Thruway, Carly
had the feeling she was simultaneously winding and un-
winding. She could feel the tensions of the city dropping
away from her. At the same time, another spring deep inside
was being wound tighter. What would she do when she saw
Brad?

She had considered surprising him. But then she'd thought
of how she would feel if she surprised him with another
woman. Just the idea of it had been enough to make her
feel as if she were dying. Picturing Brad with someone else
made her feel as though a knife were being slowly twisted
in her gut. Surprises were something that neither of them
needed at this point.

By the time she swung west on Route 17, the rain had
let up. As the clouds scudded past overhead, driven by a
stiff northwest wind, she wondered if the clearing weather
was an omen. The radio began to lose the signal, and she
explored the dial until she found something else. As the
highway curled around the first gentle slopes of the Catskills, the Carpenters sang about rainy days and Mondays
getting them down.

Carly glanced at Monticello's harness track on the way
by. A lone horse and sulky were working out on the muddy
track. Then that was behind, and Brad was closer yet.

Following directions he had sent her, Carly left Route
17 at Roscoe. Chanting the names of the towns like a litany,
she started off on the back roads, praying the valiant Valiant
up every grade. Roscoe, to Downsville, past Pepacton Res-
ervoir, to Walton, with the clouds hovering around the tops
of the mountains. Ghostly swirls of mist pirouetted around
the thick trees, spectral and mysterious. She wondered if
the headless horseman rode during the day.

The air blowing in the window was cool and damp, and
her cheeks were whipped by her hair. The wind brought the
musty scent of leaf mold, decay and life in one breath.
Apples bent the branches of gnarled trees and dotted the
ground underneath. Deer feasting on September's largess
took off at her approach.

In Franklin, she almost missed the turn to Otego. Moments later she was out of the town and back into farming

country. As she headed up the steep hill, she noticed that the clouds were breaking up and that, in the distance, a shaft of sunlight was reaching for the ground.

The road was the smallest she'd hit, and she wondered if she'd taken a wrong turn in Franklin. But not seeing any place to turn around, she kept going, following a tight right-hand curve. As she rounded the bend, she slowed. Then she stopped, her breath catching in her throat. Spread out below her to the left was the Susquehanna River valley. Almost at her feet, at least a thousand feet below, was Otego. She wasn't sure how she knew what town it was, but she did. It was Otego.

Her eyes sought out Route 7, turned left, and then right on Brad's road. Was it her imagination, or could she really see his barn?

The sun came out suddenly, in all its fresh, country glory. It was as if curtains at a theater had been drawn back, as if the stage lights had come up. Act Two, Scene One. The sun was high, angling down from the west, making the white houses in the village shine. Here and there the trees were touched with autumn, the maples glowing scarlet, the aspens yellow.

Risking life and limb, Carly shot look after look at the breathtaking view as she headed down the mountain. The road dove steeply into a hairpin turn, then curled back, and her view of the village was cut off.

She felt as if she were coming home as she crossed the bridge over the interstate, then the one over the Susquehanna. It was the bridge she and Brad had canoed under, she thought dreamily. Turning right on Route 7, she resolutely headed through the village and toward the motel. What she really wanted to do was turn left and go to Brad.

As her eyes darted from side to side, Carly wondered how the little town could feel so familiar after only one short visit. That house was where the old woman had been washing her windows. They looked nice. Had the pregnant woman who'd been weeding had her baby yet? There was the bank. Here was where Brad had picked her up the day he'd taken her to Orlo's. There was the sawmill.

As she pulled in at the motel, Carly's heart gave a leap. Then she told herself not to be ridiculous. The station wagon parked by the motel office couldn't be Brad's. There were probably hundreds like it in the area.

The Valiant died with a wheezing rattle and she leaped out of the car, still hoping that the station wagon was Brad's. Stretching to ease the stiffness in her shoulders, she looked around eagerly. Not seeing anyone, she ran lightly up the steps to the motel office.

The bell on the counter dinged politely under her palm. Nothing had changed. The same small stacks of brochures plugging Howe Caverns and the Baseball Hall of Fame sat tidily side by side. While she waited, she took a registration card and began filling it out.

"I'm sorry, miss, but there's no room at the inn," an oh-so-familiar voice said behind her.

"Brad!" Carly yelped, dropping the pen, whirling toward him.

It was the most natural thing in the world to fly to him and into his welcoming embrace. Her homecoming was complete as his lips touched hers and his arms went around her. She was crushed against him. He was there, his scent, his power, his taste. Forgetting all her vows to be cool, calm, and collected when she first saw him, she abandoned herself completely, reveled in the joy of seeing him, being in his arms.

"What are you doing here?" she asked breathlessly when they were finally able to stop kissing. She held on to him with both hands, her body pressed against his as she looked up at him. She picked out every feature, the faint laugh crinkles bracketing his eyes, the dimple in his chin, the straight line of his nose. They were all so familiar, yet at the same time they all looked new, as if put there just for her to discover all over again.

"Well, what do you think I'm doing here?" he asked wryly.

"Uh—you got flooded and had to find a place to stay?" she asked timidly.

"Haw," he guffawed, tightening his arms around her, drawing her in against his lovely, warm, welcoming strength. "I'm here because I'm waiting for you."

"For *moi?*"

"For you," he assured her tenderly, kissing her again, gently, fondly, with a hunger that was under tight control.

Suddenly remembering that the motel owner was liable

to appear at any minute, she looked around nervously. "I wonder where he is?"

"Who?"

"The owner."

"Gone fishing."

"Don't be ridiculous. He wouldn't have gone off and left the office open. Besides, he was expecting me. I have a reservation."

"No you don't. And I told him I'd lock the office when I leave."

"What are you talking about? Of course I have a reservation. And where were you? I didn't hear the door open."

"Behind it. Anyway, you can't stay here," Brad announced, looking hugely pleased with himself. "There aren't any vacancies."

"But I have a reservation."

"It was cancelled. And I've rented every room. And you can't have one."

"You can't be serious!"

"Want to bet?" he asked, and she could see in his dark, intense eyes as he looked down at her that he meant every word he'd said.

"Oh." Suddenly, she was scared. Nothing was going the way she had planned. But even so, why should she be scared? Staying with him was what she had dreamed about for weeks. The hunger in her gut was like nothing she'd ever felt before.

"Where's your luggage?"

"Where on earth do you think it is? It's in my car," she said distractedly, still trying to decide what to do.

"You'll follow me?" he asked, keeping his arm around her, moving her toward the door.

"Yes." There was no arguing with him, or with herself. She was already aching at the thought of being away from him for even a moment, and pressed herself against him.

The trip from the motel took forever. It was hard to breathe, and she had to fight to keep from nudging the nose of the Valiant against Brad's back bumper. Her hands were slippery on the worn steering wheel. She had to be totally, insanely mad to be doing this.

She was afraid the Valiant wasn't going to make it up his driveway. With a wheeze that sounded like its last gasp, the weary car clawed and scrambled over the ruts and holes. Finally, it lurched to a halt beside Brad's wagon and gave a final pitiful croak.

She clung to Brad's arm as he led the way into the house section of the barn. She took a deep breath, savoring the scent of lemon oil. She looked around, quickly picking out the features she loved so much—his works, the duck with wings spread as if drying them, the squirrels climbing—and the view out the big south windows.

Then he had her in his arms again. She plastered herself against him, as desperate for the contact as he was. There was no subtlety to the embrace, no subterfuge, no coyness. He wanted her and she wanted him, and they both knew it. They were communicating on a totally primitive level.

When he swept her up in his arms, she clung to his neck and rested her cheek contentedly against his shoulder. She didn't dare think, so she only felt. As he carried her up the stairs to the open loft, she felt his strength, felt her own desire.

He lowered her to the big bed, then sat down beside her, leaned over her, and kissed her thoroughly. Carly arched and slid one hand up and around the back of his neck as the fires roared within her. Any reservations she might have had were crisped to ashes by the heat of her hunger for him.

His hand moved up her side and conquered her aching breast. She squirmed against his grasp as he gently tested her warmth and softness with powerful fingers. Her tongue was bold, exploring his mouth. Her hand was on his thigh, and it was only a moment before she had found him and was measuring his steely hardness.

His hand left her breast, and his deft fingers were on the buttons of her trim plaid blouse. In seconds he had it open and was dealing with her bra. Her nipples stiffened at the touch of the cool air, then one burned from the heat of his palm.

His lips left hers and moved to her breast, and she moaned with pleasure. Her fingers clutched his thick black hair, urged him on as he sucked on her. She squirmed thigh against thigh and then let her legs part when his hand slid down to cup her, press against her. Digging her heels into the mattress, moving in a primitive rhythm, she thrust up against him.

His hand moved from the intersection of her thighs to her belt. Even while he was working at the buckle, she was toeing off her sneakers. Then, as he loosened her pants and shoved them down, she rolled toward him and attacked his belt, breaking a nail in her hurry. She lifted her hips so he could get her jeans down, then dragged at his, got them down and off.

She kicked to get her feet untangled, and then she was free. Brad's hand was already on her humid flesh, caressing the curly hair, heating her to the boiling point. Her fingers closed around him, and she drew at him, pulled him toward her.

For a moment they looked deep into each other's eyes, savoring the anticipation of what was to come.

He moved over her, and she welcomed him, guided him. Then she drew her hand out from between them, and he filled her. She clutched his back as he entered her. As her hips rose to welcome him, his lips were at her ear, his breath hot. He began moving.

A million years wouldn't have been long enough. As it was, their mutual hunger shortened it. Impatiently, ravenously, they celebrated their reunion in a starburst of pleasure that left them both gasping and weary, and still hungry.

Turning her head, Carly kissed his damp cheek, then rubbed her soft one against it, savoring the bristles. She didn't care if she got a beard burn. She licked him, tasted the saltiness of his sweat. Then their mouths met, and their teeth clashed in the ravenous power of their passion.

Finally, Brad brushed a damp tendril of hair back off her face. "Am I crushing you?"

"No," she whispered, loving his weight on top of her. He moved in her, and she gasped.

"Already?" she asked.

"Already," he chuckled, the sound drumming through her.

"Oh wow!" she sighed when he twitched again. She held on tight.

"Oh, Carly," he hissed hotly in her ear, his fingers digging into her back.

This time it was even more tumultuous. It was their two bodies become one. Heavenly sensations shot through Carly's body, again and again. When she thought she could bear it no more, she arched her back and moved deeply as her body was consumed in the pleasure of it all. Afterward, Brad was still there with her, holding her, snuggling her, soothing her with strokes and kisses and tender caresses while the aftershocks died slowly, peacefully.

They lay side by side on the rumpled bed, touching contentedly—hands, thighs, chests, bellies. Brad pushed her blouse back off her shoulders, and Carly unbuttoned the cuffs so she could get rid of the last of her clothing. Then she helped him get his shirt off. Now, she thought, my body is as bare to him as my soul is.

"You're beautiful," he said softly, his fingers toying with the elk's tooth that was her sole adornment.

"You're not so bad yourself," she said, grinning, combing her fingers through the hair on his chest. Beautiful? He was magnificent.

"I missed you."

"I missed you, too."

"I'm glad you came."

"I'm glad I'm here."

"How's Bambi?"

"His name isn't Bambi," she protested. "He's Pan."

"Pan was a goat," Brad pointed out reasonably.

"I don't care. I call him Pan. He's wild and primitive and beautiful, and when he gets older, he'll ravish the nymphs just like his creator does."

Brad chuckled and gave her a provocative squeeze. "I don't ravish nymphs."

"Why not? I bet it'd be fun to go running through the woods naked, laying waste to all the fair maidens."

"Running through the woods naked is a good way to get poison ivy."

"I suppose so. Well, if you get it, I'll know what you've been up to."

"The only maiden I want to lay waste to is you."

"Thank you." She ran her finger around one of his nipples.

"Something wrong?"

Unable to ignore the fear that was huddling deep inside her and knowing he could see right through her anyway, Carly nodded.

"I'm not Jason," he reminded her with a trace of exasperation. "I'm not even an artist."

"I don't think we'd better get into that," she said dryly. "How's Fred?"

"Don't ask!"

"That bad?"

"Actually, he's been on his good behavior—ever since I clobbered him with Orlo's painting."

"Maybe you finally made an impression on him."

Carly shook her head, twirling a finger in the hair on Brad's chest. "I don't think anything could make a dent in that Ivy League pomposity of his."

"Watch it!" Brad complained. "You're treading close to home."

"Ah, but you aren't pompous," she pointed out.

"I must be doing something wrong," Brad grumbled, his hands exploring her insolently.

"Whatever it is you are doing, it is not wrong," Carly assured him. "Wicked, perhaps, and definitely wanton, but not wrong. Oh my!"

"Like that?"

"You devil," Carly gasped. "Oh wow!"

"Love me," she whispered a minute later.

"Happy to oblige," he said softly, his hand probing, teasing, tantalizing. Rolling on her back, she surrendered to him, abandoned herself to pleasure. She opened herself, allowing him to explore her deepest secrets. She let him see her and feel her, let her passion show.

When the need became too great, they rolled toward each other. On their sides, they fitted together like the pieces of a jigsaw puzzle, and Carly felt whole once again. Brad's hairy leg was deliciously scratchy against the inside of her thigh. Her nipples burned against his chest. He showered her with kisses as they slowly, slowly, moved their bodies in the ancient, eternal dance.

Together, each sensing the other's need, they made it last. Pacing themselves, they paused now and then to savor their oneness. Then they moved again, climbing the stairway of ecstasy until they neared the top. Then they stopped, sliding back away from that moment, not wanting to pass the point of no return. It went on and on and on, until Carly thought maybe it would never end.

When it did, it was with a long, slow, pulsating rush that left them gasping and clinging to one another.

Later, they went downstairs to the living area. Brad grumbled when she insisted on putting on a robe, but the big open windows and bright afternoon sun made her feel vulnerable. She, who'd posed for a horde of strangers, was too shy to stay nude for him, or for the rough, naked wilderness beyond his windows. The illogic of it didn't escape her. Or him. But he didn't try to argue her out of it and politely put his robe on.

"So how's the canoe business?" she asked, taking the glass of wine he was holding out to her.

"Winding down. This is the end of the season. The river's up, though. Want to go canoeing?"

"Not today," she answered in a sultry tone.

"Haw! No. Not today," he agreed.

"Done any carving lately?"

He shook his head. "That's my wintertime amusement. Until now, that is. I have other plans for this year. Also, right now I'm busy gathering firewood and the raw materials for carving."

"Oh?"

"When I'm cutting firewood, I always keep my eye out for likely-looking pieces. Now, take this one, for example." He indicated a section of log that was occupying the space formerly held by the fawn.

"Nice," Carly said, studying its gentle curve and twists. "What's it going to be?"

"You."

Carly stared at him. "Me?"

"I want you to pose for me."

She felt a distinct chill at the idea. "I wish you hadn't said that."

"Why?" he asked, concerned.

Carly shrugged. "Maybe it's just memories. Maybe it's because I feel I'd become just an object to you."

"You know damn well—or at least you should—that you could never be that," he protested. "And I am not Jason! Hellfire—I keep telling you, I'm not even an artist!"

"So why use that corny old ploy?" Carly asked lightly.

"Because it always works," he said, grinning. "I was afraid if I relied solely on my wit, charm, and personality, I might not get you."

"What was renting every room at the motel? And did you really rent every one?"

"Every one," he assured her.

"It must have cost a fortune!"

"It wasn't too bad. Besides, the owners can use the money. And you're worth it."

"You sound like a commercial. Anyway, you could have invested your money more directly," she teased.

"I tried flattery, bribery, and usury," Brad grumbled. "Would such an unsavory direct approach have worked? You realize of course what that would make you. You're not, I hope!"

"I'm an antique dealer," she said primly.

He studied her, smiling slyly. "Same difference."

"Oh! You beast!" she said, laughing. "I walked right into that one, didn't I?" But despite her appreciation of his humor, the idea of posing made her uncomfortable and she looked at the chunk of wood he'd selected for her likeness. "Why don't you carve a—a bear or something out of it?" she asked, eyeing it nervously.

"Because I don't see a bear in it. I see you in it."

"Maybe I'm like one of those savages in New Guinea or wherever it is. Maybe I'm afraid that if you carve me, you'll capture my soul, the way they think a camera captures the soul along with the image."

"I'd like to capture your soul."

"But it's my soul!"

"Trade you," he offered with a broad, boyish smile. "You can have mine. But on second thought, since you already have it, it's not much of a trade."

There was that intensity. Why wasn't there any real vulnerability to go along with it?

"I'll settle for just your body," she responded with a lightness she didn't feel. "Now, are you going to keep my body and soul together and feed me?"

"What would you like?"

"Anything but venison."

"Perish the thought."

"Want to take another trip to Orlo's while you're here?" he asked over dinner.

"I was hoping to. And I understand there's a marvelous institution out here in the boonies called the garage sale."

"Where'd you hear about them?"

"In *The New York Times*, of course."

"Had no idea they'd reached such a lofty status."

"Huh! I'll bet one of you overintellectualized Ivy Leaguers has already done a treatise on the sociological and economic aspects of the garage sale."

"Undoubtedly, with special reference to the varied parameters inherent in the free-market system as expressed in suburban psychosexual mores. Subtitled *How to Make a Buck from Junk*."

"Anyway," she went on, "garage sales sound like just my kind of thing."

"I suppose they are," he agreed. "The peak season for them has passed, but I'm sure we can turn some up. There are always ads for them in the paper. Get enough to eat?"

"It'll keep my strength up."

"Want to bet?" he asked, reaching for her.

The river of desire began to flow again. "No." Then she grinned. "But it'll sure be fun trying to find out."

"It sure will be," he agreed, getting to his feet, drawing her up with him.

"What about the dishes?" she asked facetiously.

"To hell with the dishes," he growled, leading the way to the stairs.

In the loft, he unfastened the belt of her robe as she unfastened his. She could see the pupils of his eyes dilate as he pushed the robe back off her shoulders and let it drop to the floor. Her own eyes widened as she studied his naked body. He was a mountain of a man, tanned and hard, his belly flat, his hips trim.

Her fingers were trembling as she reached for him and gently, wonderingly, stroked his chest. They stood, inches apart, memorizing every detail of the other's body. He brushed one of her nipples with his fingertips. She shuddered, gasped, and he carefully engulfed her breast with his big, strong hand, lifting and molding the yielding flesh.

His flesh wasn't yielding. His flesh was hard, eager, and

hot. She could smell the musk of his desire. Together, they sank down on the bed. Their lips met and parted, and his tongue invaded her mouth. With one hand still fondling her breast, he slid his other over her thigh and brushed against her.

Slowly, slowly, they lay back on the bed. His hands explored her delicately, reverently, finding trigger points she'd never even read about, much less actually experienced. She let her free hand rove over his broad back until finally he drew her over on top of him. Rising, letting him see the desire she was feeling, she guided him, and sank down carefully. He reached for her breasts with both hands and gently, lovingly, tormented her.

For a time she remained still, straddling him, savoring the fullness, the closeness of him. She rested her fingertips on his hard, flat belly and grinned at him. He grinned back and blew her a kiss.

She lifted and lowered, and the pleasure began to build. Closing her eyes, she concentrated on the sensations engulfing her body. She felt him moving beneath her, in response to her, and was glad she was doing most of the work this time. She wanted to give him as much pleasure as he had given her.

His hands slid down from her breasts to her waist, and his thumbs almost met in the center of her belly, while his fingertips pressed the hollow of her spine. His grip was powerful and yet so gentle, as he guided her motions. She loved the way he led her, paced her with his dominating grasp.

She felt him pulse, and his hands stopped her, and together they hung on the brink of ecstasy. She gasped out a nervous chuckle. "You devil," she whispered as she looked down on his passion-enhanced features.

"Witch," he responded tightly, his thumbs pressing into her soft tummy, stroking her tender flesh. Then he moved her again, and she groaned with pleasure. She shifted her hips, rising and settling, stroking them both closer and closer to the peak. It was as if this was what she had been waiting for her entire life, what she had been created for.

Finally, there was no stopping either of them, and the eruptions came. Carly shuddered, wanting to collapse on

his brawny body, her own pleasure-locked muscles pre-
venting it.

At last, drained, carefully keeping her arms and legs
tangled with his so they wouldn't be parted even for an
instant, she lay forward and rolled to one side. Then, there,
in his embrace, she slid off into sleep.

Chapter Eight

As she gradually woke up, Carly had the vague feeling she was being watched. Brad's body was warm and comforting against her. She concentrated, tried to figure out what part of him was touching her. His back. It couldn't be him watching her, then. The loft was awash with the warm glow of sunlight reflecting off the natural wood surrounding them.

Slowly, languidly, still wondering why she sensed eyes on her, Carly surveyed the open beams and posts overhead. Then she picked out the hunched shape and for the longest time watched it, waiting for it to move. Only when it didn't did she realize how she'd been fooled by Brad's art. In the shadows above, the carving of the horned owl looked real.

Reassured, and thrilled as always by Brad's skill, Carly nestled closer against him. Primitive hunger began to stir within her. She shifted gently, loving the feel of his skin against hers. She slid a hand over to cup his smooth, soft hip, and then gently squeezed. He grunted softly and sighed. She felt him move and snuggled closer against his warmth.

Feeling mischievous and sexy, she slid her hand around his broad ribs. Teasingly, she combed her fingers through the thick mat of hair on his chest. Finding one of his nipples, she traced tantalizing circles around it with her nail, feeling it stiffen eagerly as she did so. Sensuously, she squirmed against his back, pressing her hips forward against his.

She licked his shoulder, tasting the faint saltiness of his sweat. He had a warm, masculine scent. She had the urge to sink her teeth into the powerful muscles at the base of his neck. Instead, she nibbled the curly hairs behind his ear, tugging gently on them with her lips.

When he shifted restlessly, reaching up to swat vaguely at her, she had to stifle a giggle. He was a sound sleeper, apparently. She slid one leg sinuously over his so she could press herself against his backside more effectively, feel him against her even more intimately. Her hips developed a life of their own that she had to restrain firmly for fear of waking him completely.

Then, unable to resist the urge any longer, Carly let her hand sneak downward from his chest. She found part of him was awake—responsive, anyway—and curled her fingers and squeezed gently. She thrilled to the intimacy of her grasp and the evidence of his subconscious desire.

Unavoidably, her body became impatient with the tantalizing game. Stretching her neck, she found the curves of his ear and blew softly. Once again, he swatted vaguely at her. But when her tongue probed, the swat became a questioning caress, an exploration, as his fingers tangled with her thick locks. She captured his earlobe between her teeth and bit gently. When he stirred, she released him.

He rolled over to face her and his lips sought hers and their mouths mingled, their tongues dueled. Her hunger became more insistent, more demanding. Side by side, they tangled their legs, then she slid her thigh over his. She moved her hips slowly, pressing against him, until her hunger could no longer be ignored. She could feel his readiness against her as she moved.

Trailing kisses over her face, he shifted, and she shifted, and they slid together as if made for each other.

"Mmmmmmmm," he purred, the sound rumbling through her as he nibbled her face.

"Good morning," she responded softly, contentedly scraping her cheek on his beard.

"It certainly is," he agreed, moving, wringing a gasp from her.

"Think so, huh?" It was hard to talk, the words coming out in jerky gasps. Her arms were around him, and she tried to fit herself against him from shoulders to ankles. His hairy chest made her nipples feel as if they were being tortured.

"Most . . . definitely," he said, moving again.

"Oh yes," she agreed, loving the feel of his belly against hers. Then talking was too much of a distraction and she clung to him, moving gently in rhythmic opposition. She squirmed, wishing she could cover him entirely, like a coat of paint. She dug her fingers into his buttock and felt him twitch.

His hands roamed over her naked back, tracing the angles of her shoulder blades, then finding the line of her spine.

He traced her backbone with a feathery stroke of his fingertips to her waist, and then lower. The insolently intimate exploration startled a gasp out of her, which only encouraged him to probe further.

They moved together in a slow, primitive rhythm. His brawny male body was against and in her soft feminine one. Wanting to totally engulf him, she curled one leg farther around him, tried to surround him completely.

It was slow, the tide of pleasure rising within her in wavelike surges. She held him closer, tighter, until at last the surf crested and broke over her, and she sank her teeth into his shoulder. She felt him shudder, felt his muscles clench as she clung to him, and rode out the turbulence of her ecstasy.

Then, as the tide receded, they lay together, sharing their closeness silently, not needing to talk. His eyes moved over her face wonderingly, as if he were seeing her for the first time. Reaching up, she brushed the thick black curls off his forehead. Gently, she smoothed his eyebrows as she tried to memorize his every feature by sight and touch.

"Good morning," he greeted her again.

"It certainly is."

"I thought that was my line."

"You want to fight?"

"I'm a lover, not a fighter," he murmured, nibbling her ear.

"You sure are."

"And I'm also human," he went on.

"Which means?"

"There are certain—ah—necessities . . ."

"Indeed," she agreed, forced at last to acknowledge her need for another kind of relief.

"Do you want to go first? Or should I?"

Carly thought for a moment. "You go first and scare away the predators."

She watched him slide out of bed and studied the play of muscles in his back as he stretched before heading for the stairs. Obviously, in addition to his carving talent, his grandfather had bequeathed him some heroic Greek blood. She could think of several classical Greek statues Brad might have been the model for.

Finally, feeling incredibly, bonelessly relaxed, but goaded

by her body's needs, she slid out of bed. She looked down at her robe, which lay in a tangle beside his on the floor. The thought of being enfolded in the scratchy terry cloth just didn't appeal to her. Emboldened by his casual lack of modesty, she put a tentative hand on the banister and started down. The sun was warm on her bare body as she descended.

"You sure you don't want to model for me?" he asked as, emerging from the bathroom, he surveyed her.

She treated him to a similar survey. "Maybe. If you agree to pose for me."

He met her at the bottom of the stairs and drew her close. "I have no objection."

"I'll have to think about it," she said thoughtfully.

"How could it go wrong, with me as your subject?" He grinned, releasing her. "What would you like for breakfast?"

"Coffee for me, and humble pie for you?" she called as she closed the bathroom door behind her. He muttered something inaudible in response.

She was adjusting the shower when there was a loud knock on the door. "Yes?" she asked, opening the door a crack and peeking around it in a coy display of false modesty.

"Coffee," he explained unnecessarily, handing her a steaming mug. He cocked an ear at the sound of the shower. "Haven't you heard there's a terrible water shortage?"

"There is?" she asked, worried. Then she noticed the gleam in his eye. "Save water and shower with a friend? Is that the idea?"

"Of course," he agreed, pushing the door open, easily overcoming her token resistance.

Like everything else he had, the tub was unique—a wood barrel six feet across, two feet deep. It was a bath of rural, imaginative, practical luxury. In moments they were sharing it, twisting and turning under the spray from two shower heads, their coffee cups resting on the ledge out of the line of the showers, but within easy reach.

"Now this is definitely a bath to be shared," Carly observed.

"Sure is," he agreed, reaching for her.

"I mean, this tub," she retorted, enjoying the wet, slick

feel of his warm body. She loved the way she had to crane her head back to look up at him. "I'll bet you've shared it with hundreds of women."

"Thousands," he corrected solemnly.

"Beast," she growled, pounding his hard chest with her fists.

Without any effort at all, he captured them both in one hand and then proceeded to kiss her thoroughly. "Are you going to stand around in here until you look like a prune?" he asked when he was done, "or would you like some breakfast?"

"All I ever have is coffee," she answered a little breathlessly.

"Well, that's not enough for me. I won't be good for a thing if I don't get something in me."

"You've already been good for a great deal. Very good," Carly purred as she reached for the soap. "Wash my back?"

"Only your back?" he asked, cocking a hopeful eyebrow at her.

"If you want to get out of here and get some breakfast..."

"I think maybe breakfast can wait."

"I think maybe it can," she agreed, gasping as he began soaping her thighs enthusiastically.

"No. On second thought, I don't think so," he added.

"You beast!"

"Of course. Come on, you wanton redhead, get a wiggle on."

"Okay, spoilsport," she grumbled.

As she dried off, her stomach began informing her in no uncertain terms that coffee alone was not going to do. Amazing the way other appetites take a back seat to the need for food, she thought absently as she joyously contemplated an entire day with Brad.

Working together in the kitchen, they managed to get a meal assembled in spite of a tendency to bump into each other frequently. They ate in front of his huge picture windows, sunlight washing over them.

Finally she sat back, sated. "You're going to destroy my figure," she observed.

"Now that would be felony vandalism," he observed,

surveying her with a smile. "Don't worry, I'll work it off you."

"You are as randy as a goat!" she protested.

"Not what *I* meant at all," he responded with lofty innocence. "*I* was thinking of a walk in the woods."

"Oh." Carly made a face at him. "Sounds nice."

"On the other hand . . ."

"I'll go get dressed," she said quickly before he could continue.

Once outside, Carly inhaled deeply, tried to embrace the brisk fall day with her entire body. Overhead, the sky was a perfect blue. A few puffy white clouds sailed before a strong northwest wind. Everything was fresh and alive and bright. The maple trees along the road were touched with scarlet from the light frost that had followed the rain. The world had never looked better. She'd never felt better. Brad had pressed enough scrambled eggs, sausage, and English muffins on her to last her a week.

"Where on earth do you get the incredible hulks you drive up here?" Brad asked as he took her hand.

She eyed the faded Valiant affectionately. It was, after all, the car that had gotten her to Otego. To Brad. "I've got a cut-rate rental place where I get them," she explained.

"Cut-rate? They should pay you to take them," he protested good-naturedly.

"It got me here."

"For which I will be eternally grateful," he assured her. "But please, promise me you'll never do it again."

"Do what? Come up here?"

"Rent a wreck like that. Scares me to death, thinking of you driving it. Looks like an accident looking for a place to happen. As for coming up here, I don't want you ever to leave!"

Carly felt a glow of pleasure at his remark, but also a twinge of fear. "Let's not mention leaving."

"Suits me. You going to be warm enough?"

"I've got a jacket," she answered, digging into her pocket for the key to the Valiant.

"You locked your car?" he asked incredulously.

"City reflexes," she explained, dragging out the red down vest she'd gotten for an abortive ski trip to Hunter Mountain two years before.

He reached for her hand again as soon as she had the vest on, then guided her around the corner of the barn and down the hill below the deck. Following the tracks made by his station wagon, they pushed through the tall weeds. A flock of small birds scattered in front of them, dancing like dry leaves in a high wind.

Brad stopped suddenly. "Listen," he urged softly.

Carly listened. At first all she heard was the sound of the wind in the bare trees. Then a new sound intruded—distant, mysterious, lonely. At first she thought it was hounds baying.

"Geese," Brad explained, scanning the sky.

Tilting her head back, Carly searched the cloud-flecked dome of blue. The distant, wild honking was louder now. It seemed to come from everywhere, so her ears were no use in locating the source.

"There they are."

Carly followed the line of his arm, but for a long time saw nothing. Then she picked them out, a ragged v, black dots flickering with silver as the sun caught them. The lines of the v wavered, and she watched with concern as one laggard struggled to catch up.

It was one of the most beautiful things she'd ever seen in her life. It seemed to touch a chord deep in the Indian portion of her soul. She felt a longing to be with the distant geese, to be as wild and free as they were.

After the flock had become tiny specks in the distance and their cries could no longer be heard, she and Brad resumed their walk.

"You own all this?" Carly asked as they climbed through a field. The hay had been cut to ankle height.

"Yep. I own about a hundred acres."

"What do you use it for?"

"Use it for?" he asked. "Why would I want to use it?"

"Don't you farm it or anything?"

He shook his head. "I have a neighbor come in to cut the hay. And I harvest firewood for myself. In a way, I do use it. I enjoy it."

Carly thought this over. "I like that," she decided.

"Well, your great-grandmother would have approved."

"You trying to impress her?" Carly asked, shooting him a sharp glance.

"I have the feeling she's always with us," he answered, reaching over to touch the elk tooth.

"So do I. In fact..."

"In fact what?" Brad asked when her voice trailed off.

"Oh, it's stupid."

"If it's coming from you, it can't be," he protested.

Grateful for his encouragement, she smiled. "I was just thinking. Until recently, I haven't felt that way. Like she's with me, I mean."

She moved closer to Brad and felt like she was on cloud nine when he promptly slid his arm around her. She tucked her hand in the back pocket of his jeans and rested her head against his shoulder as they continued up the hill. She felt his lips brush her hair.

"I guess I sort of lost her there for a while," Carly went on, continuing her train of thought.

"When you stopped trying to be an artist," Brad suggested.

She gave him an annoyed sock in the ribs. "You're too smart for your own good, you know that?"

"Sorry." He was silent a moment, and there was only the sound of their feet rustling through the dry weeds. "When did you find her again?"

Carly thought back. She'd only just realized that for a while she had lost her wonderful ancestress. When had she rediscovered her? "I think it was about the time I met you," she decided at last. "Maybe when we went canoeing."

"Which goes to show we belong together. Now all we have to do is get you out of the city and back to your art work and she'll be happy."

"Why can't you be the artist?"

"Because I build canoes and paddles," he countered.

"But..."

"I carve for myself, for my own pleasure," he went on.

"There's no reason for you not to."

He shook his head. "I never sell my carvings. I give them to people I know love them."

"Like my fawn."

"Like your fawn. Like the fox I gave to Thompson's. They're priceless."

"They are," she agreed.

"But not the way you mean," he responded calmly. "I

mean, literally, that they are priceless. They cannot be priced. What I mean is that if I started to make them for any kind of monetary reason, the magic would go out of it for me. You can't put a value on something you love."

Carly hugged him close, moved by the depth of his feeling. Then she shrouded her own intense emotion with humor. "You realize, of course, where this leaves a dealer like me?"

"And good riddance!" he replied, smiling.

"Beast!" Carly growled, punching him in his rock-hard stomach.

"Animal," he retorted, swinging her around in front of him with an effortless sweep of his arm.

"Monster," she whispered as he drew her against him, lifting her, holding her tight.

"Witch," he hissed as his mouth covered hers.

Curling her arms around his neck, she hung from him, balancing precariously on one toe as they devoured each other. His hands dug into her, one bruising the small of her back, the other slipping lower, cupping her, grinding her against him. Willingly, eagerly, she abandoned herself to him.

"Your attitude is admirable," Carly admitted grudgingly after they broke the kiss, "but not terribly practical."

"My attitude toward dealers?" he asked, grinning down at her.

"No! I mean your attitude about selling your carvings, you lecherous philistine."

They headed deeper into the woods. "My attitude is hardly that of a philistine."

"Okay, I'll concede that point. What I mean is, you are passing up the opportunity to make money."

"Money isn't everything."

"No, but . . ."

"I make enough to pay my bills," he went on. "And I could make more if I wanted to build more canoes. Of course, the quality would suffer . . ."

"Oh, don't *ever* do that!"

He gave her an affectionate squeeze. "Don't worry, I won't. Anyway, I build only as many as I want to—ten to fifteen a year. And that provides me with a very comfortable existence."

"Only ten a year? How much do you sell them for, anyway?" Carly asked, doing some quick mental arithmetic.

"Between fifteen hundred and three thousand dollars each, depending on how much customizing I do."

Carly let out a loud whistle. "The Rolls-Royce of canoes," she commented. "Why do people pay so much?"

"I have a few little secrets that make mine faster than anyone else's—so far, at least. I found an unusual way to put my hydraulic engineering knowledge to work."

"Oh!" Carly was relieved to hear his education hadn't been entirely squandered.

He shot her a wry grin when she blurted out what she'd been thinking. "And I also tailor each one to the individual customer."

"Tailor them?"

"I adjust the seats and the hull shape, depending on the weight and strength of the paddlers."

"I had no idea it was so technical."

"It's not, really. Most of what I do is just seat-of-the-pants tinkering."

"Having a sudden attack of modesty?"

"Nope. It's just that I enjoy it so much I have a hard time thinking of it as work—even though I do earn my living from it."

Their footsteps were noisy on the dry leaves. Around them the woods were quiet, and Carly wondered where the animals were.

"We're making too much noise," Brad explained when she asked. "The animals are here, but to them we sound like a herd of elephants."

"Oh."

"If you want to see wildlife, what you have to do is sit very quietly. After about fifteen minutes the animals forget you're here, or decide that you're harmless, and start to come out."

Carly rubbed her arms. Here, in the shade of the woods, it wasn't as warm as she'd expected. "I think we'd better keep moving. Is this where you get your firewood? I don't see any stumps or anything."

"I try to be as tidy as possible. I cut the stumps off as close to the ground as I can. And then, any brush that's left, I pile up for small animals to use for cover."

"Very thoughtful."

"I try to be," he murmured, looking down at her fondly.

"Great-grandma would have loved you," Carly noted, squeezing his arm.

"I like to think so."

"You're not just saying all these things to impress me, are you?"

"What do you think I am, an antique dealer?"

"Oh! Are you going to get it!" Carly made a fist and waved it threateningly in his face.

"I already have," he responded wickedly, grabbing her fist, prying her fingers open, and tenderly kissing her palm.

"Oh, you," she growled, grinning.

"Careful, watch where you step," he cautioned suddenly, pulling her to one side.

"What? Oh!"

"Hello there, little fellow," Brad said softly. "You're out late in the season." Stooping, he gently scooped up a bright orange and black butterfly that she had been about to step on.

"A butterfly?" Carly asked.

"A monarch." The dainty insect clung to his finger with hair-thin legs, slowly opening and closing its wings.

Carly was afraid to breathe, afraid she'd blow the butterfly off Brad's hand. "What's it doing here this time of year?"

Brad inspected it closely. "Late bloomer, I guess. It's one of this year's hatchings."

"How can you tell?"

"Look how fresh and bright the colors are. The wings don't have any nicks or tears in them, either. Must have come out of its cocoon within the last day or two. It's probably on its way south."

"I didn't know they migrated."

Brad nodded. "Monarchs are about the only ones that do." He lifted his hand, and as if it understood, the butterfly took flight, rising in a shaft of sunlight, looking like a bit. of stained glass as it danced upward.

"There's a valley in Central America where they gather over the winter, thousands and thousands of them," Brad went on as they resumed their walk.

"Think he'll make it?" Carly asked worriedly, hugging Brad's arm.

"There's a favoring wind. There's a good chance he will."

"You could carve a pin like him," Carly suggested as they walked on.

"So you could sell thousands of them?"

"That's not what I meant!" she protested. "I wasn't even thinking of that."

"Sorry," Brad apologized.

"I'm not as crass and mercenary as you seem to think."

"I said I was sorry. Want to go canoeing this afternoon?"

"It's a little chilly for a swim," Carly pointed out, rubbing her arms.

"I didn't say a thing about tipping," Brad retorted. "Unless, of course, you lack confidence—or ability," he added teasingly.

Carly shot him a glare of mock anger. "What I'm confident of is that I can match *you* stroke for stroke."

"Oh, is that so?" he asked in a soft, seductive tone, his hand sliding down to cup her bottom intimately.

She gave her hips a lascivious twitch. "That's so," she retorted smugly before leaning into him and giving him a hug.

"How brave are you feeling?" he asked as they turned to head back in the direction they'd come.

"Why do you ask?"

"I'm just wondering how much of a taste of river canoeing I should give you."

"Is it really dangerous?"

Brad frowned and thought for a moment. "It can be challenging."

"So challenge me," Carly responded promptly.

"We'll need two cars."

"Why?"

"Because the challenging parts we don't do going upstream. We'll leave one car at our projected landing point, and drive back to get the other. Unless you are feeling very strong. Like paddling up the rapids."

"I'll pass on that. So what will we do for a second car?"

"That wreck of yours will do if I can cobble up a canoe carrier for it."

"So let's get going," Carly said as they emerged from the woods. She was eager to try something besides the placid stretch of river they'd done before. And for some reason, she was also eager to show Brad that she could handle anything he threw at her.

Chapter Nine

LEAVING THE SHABBY Valiant in the parking lot of the small grass-strip airpark just north of Oneonta, Carly switched over to Brad's brawny wagon. She'd carefully followed him all the way from his house, up Route 7, through Oneonta, then off on a one-lane dirt road to the airpark. The canoe was on the roof rack.

From the airpark they headed farther north along the river. As she studied what little she could see of it, Carly began to feel disappointed. It didn't look any harder than the stretch around Otego. Then they passed a fifty-foot-high concrete dam. That was another kettle of fish entirely. What if they by mistake went over it? They'd be killed.

"Goodyear Dam," Brad explained. "Canadian company uses it to generate power. We portage around it."

At a little town called Portlandville, they pulled up beside a large expanse of calm water.

"This looks peaceful enough," Carly noted as she helped load the paddles into the canoe. "What is it?"

"Goodyear Lake. The Susquehanna is backed up here by Goodyear Dam. It isn't like this once we get below the dam, so get your life jacket on," he added as he slipped into his.

"Why?" Carly asked as she followed suit. "I'm a good swimmer."

"I don't doubt it. Here, let me get that." He helped her adjust the laces so the foam-filled vest fitted snugly. "But in the first place, the water is on the chilly side and life jackets help protect against hypothermia. And in the second, the currents can be strong and tricky. And no matter how good a swimmer you are, if you end up in the water, you need all the help you can get."

"Currents?"

"This is a river," he pointed out dryly as they slid the canoe into the water.

"I know it's a river. But what I've seen of it so far hasn't looked like much."

"And the blind man who grabbed the elephant's tail thought the whole animal was built like a rope," Brad retorted. "Come on, Tecumapese. You're in for an education today."

Their starting point was a small cove at the upper end of the lake. As they paddled through the reeds at the entrance, Carly compared the bargelike Grumman aluminum they were in with the light, responsive racing canoe they had been in before. The Grumman felt heavy and clumsy. In Brad's, all it took was a touch of paddle to water to send them skimming along. She'd wanted to take the racing canoe, but he'd insisted they use the more stable aluminum one.

Swinging to the right, they headed down a channel that rapidly opened out to a huge expanse of clear water. Judging by how far they'd come since the dam, it couldn't be the main part of the lake. Brad had put her in the stern, and she was able to admire the breadth and strength of the muscles in his back and shoulders as he paddled. Heading where he indicated, hugging the left shore with its stiff ranks of cattails, Carly put more power into her strokes.

The strange racing paddle made it hard to steer. In lake canoeing she'd learned to keep a straight course by using a J stroke, twisting the paddle and pushing it away from the canoe every two or three strokes. With the wide, bent racing paddle, such a motion was almost impossible, so she tried Brad's method, steering by calling switches from one side to the other. It took a while and a good deal of weaving around, but she finally got the hang of it.

Brad helped them round a point to the left by bow-ruddering. Then they cut across toward the right and rounded another point. Ahead of them lay a long, straight stretch of water about two hundred yards wide. On both sides, heavy woods sloped down steeply to the water.

Soon the channel opened out again and vacation cottages and docks again dotted the shore. Brad maintained his pace with machinelike steadiness, dipping and thrusting his paddle, driving the canoe forward with every stroke.

Carly assumed they must now be in the main part of the lake. She wondered how much farther it was to the dam. Her shoulders were starting to ache. Not about to complain, mindful of the way Brad challenged her at every opportunity, Carly matched him stroke for stroke. The ache in her shoulders grew steadily worse and soon became agonizing, but she kept paddling. Switching often eased the discomfort. Then the pain spread—to the small of her back and her thighs.

After another ten minutes, to her surprise and relief, the pain began to fade. Her muscles had warmed to the task, and she was soon feeling better than ever. Brad, too, seemed to get his second wind as they crossed a broad expanse of water lined with houses and small yards. She was glad he knew where he was going. The lake had an infinite number of coves that all looked alike to her. She was sure, despite the map he'd given her, she would have chosen the wrong one and spent hours wandering around looking for the dam.

Finally, Brad guided them under a steel cable supported by white steel drums. Ahead, the lake appeared to drop off into nothingness, and Carly could hear the rush of water down the face of the dam. If she hadn't been with Brad and trusted him as much as she did, she would have called it quits right then. She kept imagining being swept over the dam, plunging fifty feet to her death.

To her relief, Brad hugged the left shore and guided them to a landing at the base of a monster concrete buttress of some sort. Twenty feet away, she could see the water streaming over the curving concrete lip of the dam, and heard its thundering roar as it hit the bottom. Feeling definitely queasy, she stepped onto the steep bank and helped Brad pull the canoe up out of the water.

"Here we go," he ordered, bending to pick up the canoe.

Carly looked up the bank, a twisting, muddy path climbing at least twenty feet over roots and around rocks. "Up there?" she asked dubiously.

Brad's grin was wicked, daring her to back down. "Yup."

Carly took a deep breath and bent to pick up her end of the canoe. "Let's go." As she lifted, she wished again they'd used Brad's canoe rather than the Grumman. His weighed half what this one did.

Her sneakers skidding on the mud, Carly scrambled after Brad, trying desperately to keep her end of the canoe under control and not let it go smashing onto a rock. It felt as though her arms were being pulled out of their sockets, and she was beginning to think they'd never reach the top, when, suddenly, they did. Woods surrounded them, the colorful fall leaves fluttering down as they lost their grip on the trees. The water over the dam provided a deep, thundering background.

"Need a breather?" he asked as he eased the canoe down.

"I could use one," she admitted, relieved she hadn't been forced to ask.

"We're going to have to get you in shape," Brad observed as he stretched the kinks out of his shoulders.

"I'm in good shape," Carly panted. "I swim at least twice a week at the Y."

"Your shape is fine," he agreed, surveying her with obvious relish. "It's your conditioning I'm talking about."

"I'm in good condition," she insisted, wondering if she dared sit down for a minute.

"Oh? You really think so?"

"Yes. I'm in good condition. I'm just not in great condition, like you are."

"Well, you'll need to be in great condition next spring," he noted, bending to pick up the canoe again.

"I will be," she assured him grimly. If they didn't finish the race, it sure wasn't going to be because of her.

The trip down was worse than the one up had been. Now they had to cover not only the twenty feet they had scrambled up, but the fifty-foot height of the dam. The track was more a gorge than a path.

At one point Carly slipped to one knee and the canoe smashed down on a rock with a resounding boom. Brad shot her a concerned, questioning look. She quickly checked to make sure that the canoe wasn't damaged, and then grinned apologetically. She was glad the roar of the water made conversation impossible, so she didn't have to hear some choice comment from him on clumsiness.

To her relief, they rested again at the bottom. She eyed the rushing torrent dubiously, regretting her earlier comments about how tame the river looked. The water swept down the face of the dam in a smooth sheet, then shattered against the rocks. Bouncing and foaming, it had quieted a little where they stood, but was still swirling past at a terrifying rate.

"This is why I insisted on the Grumman," Brad explained, his lips close to her ear so she could hear him.

Carly nodded nervously.

He hit her with his dashing, flashing grin. "Got to go for it now," he bellowed. "I'm not about to lug this barge back up that damn cliff."

Carly looked back the way they'd come and nodded. She couldn't possibly face that again.

"Don't try to do much steering," he warned as she scrambled into the stern again, bending close to her so she could hear him. "I'll handle that from the bow. You just paddle like hell. We either go faster than the current or slower. Otherwise it'll twist us sideways. I'll call the switches. Don't worry about both of us paddling on the same side, and don't switch unless you hear me yell. Okay?"

"Okay," she agreed as he leaned close.

"If we should go over, don't try to hold on to the canoe, I'll worry about that. And don't try to swim against the current. Get over on your back and head downstream feet first so you don't crash your head into anything. Once you're under control, angle toward the bank. Got it?"

"You're not very reassuring," she responded dryly over the roar of the water.

He cupped the back of her head with his hand and he gave her a quick, lusty kiss. "You're gonna love it," he assured her, grinning broadly.

"Oh, sure," she muttered dubiously as he stepped into the bow and picked up his paddle. She eyed the swift current warily. There were rocks all over, and she couldn't imagine how they were going to miss them all. Resolutely, she clamped down on her fear and reminded herself that Brad had done this countless times and must know what he was doing.

All too suddenly they were off and away. Carly paddled for all she was worth, trying desperately to make the canoe move faster than the water. They bounced and pitched in the haystack waves kicked up from the rocks, all of which they miraculously missed. Furiously, she paddled, blinking as cold spray stung her face. She saw Brad swing his paddle from right to left, and switched sides quickly in response to his bellowed *"Hut!"*

They passed the outflow from the generators, a powerful thrust of water shoving them to the left of the rushing river.

Brad called a switch without changing himself, and the canoe angled swiftly to the right. Then he switched without calling "Hut," and they were paddling on opposite sides again as they swept down between two huge rocks. The current shot them along. Water was foaming angrily around them.

There was no time to breathe, rest, or even think. All Carly could do was paddle and try not to miss any of Brad's signals. The canoe had become a mad toboggan, plunging down the river on the bare edge of control. Brad handled his paddle with deft ease, flipping it from side to side, sometimes calling for her to switch, sometimes not. The muscles in his shoulders bulged as he dug in the blade, pulling hard to keep the canoe moving fast enough.

Carly could feel the current grab them and knew she didn't dare let up. She was aware of the water trying to twist the canoe sideways. If it succeeded, she knew they'd be doomed. The keel would catch and they'd be over in an instant.

They swept down on a low bridge and were under it before she'd really noticed it. Here, at least, the river was a little more open and there seemed to be fewer rocks. Ahead, to the left, it looked wider and slower. She was just starting to relax a little when, to her surprise, Brad ruddered, angling them sharply to the right, away from the quiet open water ahead. There was a mad swoop and a rush as they bulleted down a narrow chute between a small island and the right bank, the water rushing them along at an insane pace, the bank whipping past, almost catching her paddle, they were so close.

Carly glanced back and discovered why Brad had gone to the right instead of the left. The trunk of a huge fallen tree was blocking the entire channel from the island to the left bank. If they'd gone that way, they would have wound up in a cul-de-sac. Because of the bend in the river, the obstacle couldn't be seen until it was too late to change course.

A few hundred yards later the river did slow and widen out, and Carly heaved a sigh of relief. She kept paddling, but not as hard as she had been. Brad twisted around and shot her a triumphant grin. She grinned back.

Exhilarated, her strength multiplied tenfold, her paddle

light as a feather, she dug it into the water. There wasn't anything that needed to be said. She was more in touch with Brad now than at any time other than during their love-making. She knew somehow she was feeling what he was feeling, that he was feeling what she was feeling. They were one, together, as they paddled on.

The world seemed deserted. The banks of the river were unsullied by houses or people. Occasionally an electric line would cross overhead, but aside from that they might have been in virgin wilderness.

Then bridges intruded, three of them. One was a low iron one for a back road, while further on was a pair on towering concrete pilings. There were signs of bank beaver and muskrat. They rounded a curve and startled a great blue heron into flight. His broad wings stroking powerfully, his head bobbing at the end of his long, sinuous neck, he tried to gain altitude.

Rounding another bend, Carly felt the current grab them again, and wondering if they were facing another suicidal plunge, pulled harder to stay ahead of it. To her regret, the river remained straight and clear. They passed a few shabby cottages on the left and a small parking lot and launching site on the right, and then slid beneath another small bridge.

The current eased, and Brad guided them over close to the left-hand shore. Within a quarter of a mile they had reached the airpark, and he headed them into the muddy bank and stepped out, his sneaker disappearing in the mud as he grabbed the canoe and steadied it. Beyond, Carly could see where a large stream came in from the left. There was a ruffled stretch of shallow water beyond. She was acutely disappointed that they had to stop here. She wanted to keep on going forever.

At the same time, though, the heaviness in her arms warned her of just how tired she was. She waited while Brad dragged the canoe halfway up the bank with her still in it, then gratefully let him help her out. Wearily, she trudged up the grassy slope and looked around for the Valiant. She finally spotted it over by the hangars, about five hundred miles away. She thought of lugging the canoe all that way and decided to study the river while she rested a bit.

"Let me have the keys and I'll go get the car," Brad offered, not at all taken in by her sudden interest in the river.

"I could do it," she protested with as much heat as she could summon, digging into her pocket for the keys.

"I'm sure you could. Don't go away."

"Not likely," she sighed to herself as he walked off. She stretched out and put the life jacket behind her head as a pillow. Every muscle in her body seemed to let out a huge sigh of relief and relax all at once. Folding her hands across her stomach, she stared up at the few puffy clouds in the sky, watching them as they sailed along on the wind.

She heard the car approaching but didn't even twitch as it pulled up beside her. Instead, she remained flat on her back until Brad was towering over her, silhouetted against the bright sky.

"I can't move," she informed him solemnly. "I think I'm paralyzed."

"Really? You look okay to me."

"Go away and let me die in peace."

"On your feet," he ordered, reaching down with one hand to help.

"Oh my goodness," she groaned as she let him haul her up.

"Let's get the canoe," he urged.

"Let's not and say we did," she argued feebly, following him. He didn't seem the least bit tired, and it galled her.

Somehow, she managed to help him get the canoe up on the roof of her car. In a few seconds they had it strapped down, resting on the foam blocks he'd clamped on the gunwales. Taking the keys from him, she slid behind the wheel, determined to carry on somehow. She knew they still had to retrieve his car before they could head for home—his home—and she could collapse completely.

"How far did we paddle, anyway?" she asked as they passed the hangars.

"Eight miles. Maybe a little more."

"Eight miles?" she asked, dismayed.

"What's the matter?"

"I'm exhausted, that's what's the matter," she retorted. "And now you tell me we covered only a tenth of the race?"

"About that," he agreed.

"Maybe you'd better start lining up another partner," she suggested reluctantly.

"Fiddlesticks," he snorted, looking over at her, reaching across to give her shoulder a reassuring squeeze. The feel of his hand on her rekindled her strength, and she managed to smile at him. "We'll have you in shape by next spring. We've got all winter to train for it. Then there are the Little Red Caboose race and the Phelps Hose Company race as tune-ups, too."

"Are you sure you *really* want me as your partner?"

He looked over at her with intense sincerity. "I was never surer of anything in my life."

"Why?"

"Why am I sure?"

"No. Why me?"

"Because you're there?" he joked.

"Be serious," she grumbled, turning right on Route 7 to head up to Portlandville and his car.

"Why do I want you to be my partner?" he asked himself, apparently taking the question quite seriously. "Because you'll be great at it. Because this is something I want to share with you. Because I think I love you."

Carly felt a jolt at his choice of words. "What did you say?"

"I think I love you," he repeated softly.

"Oh," she said in a very small voice.

"Is that all you have to say? 'Oh'?"

"I—don't know what else to say."

"Don't you believe me?"

"It's just that it's so fast. We hardly know each other."

"We do in the Biblical sense."

"I didn't mean that."

"Doesn't going to bed with me mean anything?"

Carly had the feeling everything had been turned all around. "Wait a minute," she protested. "I'm the one who's supposed to say I love you and you're the one who's supposed to assure me that you love me, too."

"So why don't you?" he challenged, smiling.

"Why don't I what?" Carly was totally bewildered and wondered if it was just because she was so tired.

"Tell me you love me?"

"I . . ." The words stuck in her throat.

"Don't you?" he asked.

"I don't know," she admitted unhappily.

It was his turn to answer with a soft "Oh."

"Well, you hardly seem sure of it yourself," she pointed out in exasperation. "You only said you *think* you love me."

"That's right," he agreed calmly. He was stroking the back of her neck, his strong fingers beneath the thick waves of her hair. She wanted desperately to lean her head against his hand, feel the strength and warmth of his palm against her cheek.

"You're not sure," she plowed on determinedly, wondering as she did so if she was deliberately trying to crush the insane hope his statement had triggered.

"Don't you realize that *I love you* are the three easiest words there are for a man to say?"

"No. I never discussed the subject with my brothers."

Brad nodded. "When a man wants a woman, physically, as much as I want you, it's a very easy thing to say, a very simple lie to tell. A man's glands can drive him to incredible falsehoods. Often, he lies to himself as much as he does to the woman."

"So it's only your glands talking," Carly said, trying to make her voice light.

"I'm trying to figure out just what it is that's talking," Brad admitted, still fondling the back of her neck, making her feel all soft and tender and hungry in spite of her weariness.

"Well, I know that my glands are answering."

"What about your heart?"

"I don't know," she temporized, looking over at him, and felt herself melting just at the sight of him. She wrenched her attention back to her driving. "What about yours?"

"What do you think I've been saying all this time?" he asked indignantly. "I don't know!"

"Why do I have the feeling this conversation isn't going anywhere?" Carly asked as she pulled off the road near Brad's station wagon.

"Probably because it isn't," he answered wryly. "I think I may have made a fool of myself."

"Don't worry about it," Carly said lightly.

"Want to move the canoe over to my car?" he asked as he started to get out.

"I don't think I have the strength. It'll be all right on mine, won't it?"

"Should be. I'll check the straps. Pull over if you notice it shifting at all. I'll be right behind you. Think you can find your way back to my place all right?"

"Like a homing pigeon," she assured him. "And, Brad?"

"Yeah?" he asked, pausing before he closed the door of her car.

"If you want to go on making a fool of yourself, I don't mind at all."

"Thanks," he answered, grinning.

A few minutes later she was back on the road, heading south toward Oneonta. In her rearview mirror she could see Brad following her. She was torn, wishing he was with her and glad that he wasn't so she had a chance to think.

His announcement had stunned her. He was so blunt, so honest. She'd never known a man like him before. There was no subterfuge to him at all.

But he wasn't shallow. What was that expression? Still waters run deep. Beneath that calm exterior of his, he ran very deep—turbulent, even. He was as complex as the river he loved to paddle.

She was still wrestling with the problem as she guided the Valiant up his rocky driveway. She switched the motor off and listened as it gave its usual death rattle. Brad pulled up alongside just as she was getting out.

Wordlessly, they slipped their arms around each other's waists as they made their way up to the house. She leaned against his strength, glad for the support she found there, and not just because of her physical exhaustion.

"Hungry?" he asked as they emerged into his spacious living room.

"Ravenous."

"Get yourself a glass of wine or something while I get the barbecue going."

"As beat as I am, if I have wine on an empty stomach, I'll conk out in about thirty seconds."

"Better skip the wine, then. I don't feel like spending the evening alone. Can you hold out till I get the barbecue going?"

"I'll try."

"Never mind, a broiler will do fine. Give me fifteen minutes before you start chewing on the furniture."

With her helping, it was more like half an hour before they were ready to sit down to dinner. Something about her presence slowed the preparations. He kept grabbing her at every opportunity, and she did her best to provide as many opportunities as she could.

The hamburgers were divine. The cheap red wine out of a gallon jug was the nectar of the gods. The last of the tomatoes from his garden were red and sweet. Though as far as she was concerned, it could have been anything so long as it was food. She didn't remember the last time she had been so hungry.

She was glad, too, that they were too busy eating to resume their earlier conversation. She just wanted to feel, to experience being with him, sharing his company. She didn't want to explore the complex feelings that were threatening her. Hope, fear, and doubt were all jumbled together. She wasn't even sure how she wanted to feel about him. And she was definitely afraid of finding out. She was afraid of just how she did feel about him.

When the meal was finished, she let him help her to her feet. Her hand in his, she followed him to the stairs with child-like willingness, but not innocence. Her heart was beating very quickly as he escorted her to the sleeping loft. He drew her into his arms and she abandoned herself to the warmth and security his embrace gave her. She let herself feel his body against hers.

He undressed her tenderly, as if she were as fragile as a butterfly. He exposed her, and his hands roamed, worshiping her reverently. She stood before him, let him tantalize himself, and her, with his caresses.

Then he eased her down on the bed and stood over her for a moment before he began to undress. She watched the flex and play of his muscles as he shed his shirt. He loosened his belt and shoved his pants down, and the sight of him so bold, so eager and ready, increased her hunger for him. She reached for him as he sank down onto the bed beside her.

She stroked his cheek as she welcomed his kiss. Then she explored his back, outlined the muscles she'd watched all afternoon. His mouth moved from her lips to her throat, then lower to capture one of her nipples. His teeth and tongue teased her into searing flames, making her toss her head in ecstasy as she tangled her fingers in his thick, black curly locks.

He slid lower, and his tongue found the hollow of her navel, wringing a gasp from her. And lower, until she moaned with pleasure at his intimate kiss. She opened herself wide to him, and he responded by devouring her until she became nearly delirious.

Finally, he abandoned that pursuit and turned and slid up along her. She drew him over her, hugged him as he filled her. She fastened her mouth on his and clutched his back, her hips rising in welcome. Then she twined her legs around his, and they rested, pressing hard against each other.

"I thought you were tired," he whispered as they lay interlocked on the huge bed.

"I'm exhausted. But something rekindled my energy."

"I'm glad," he said softly.

"So am I."

He moved, and she answered, her body moving in provocative ways, so wantonly that it surprised her. It felt as if they had been choreographed, matched by the careful stroke of a benevolent providence. It was ecstasy like she had never felt before. Every time it seemed better, more fitting, more wonderful.

Once again they climbed the glorious heights together. For a long, long time they clutched each other, trying to maintain the peak. Then they slumped with exhaustion. She felt him showering her with kisses and caresses as she lay beneath him. Finally, she managed to squirm enough to ease him off so they lay side by side, but still entwined.

"It's been a good day," Brad said softly as he slid a pillow under her head.

"Very good," she agreed, nibbling his raspy chin. "Is much of the river like the part below the dam?"

"It varies. There's a stretch a little past where we took out today that eats canoes."

"Really?"

"Last year during the Seventy, four or five got chewed up there."

"Why's it so bad?"

"It's fast, and there's an abandoned railroad trestle, a monstrosity that creates a whirlpool when the water's high. There's always a mess of fallen trees and snags there, too."

"Is it dangerous for people as well as canoes?"

"If you don't know what you're doing, it can be. You game to try it?"

She nodded and stroked her fingers through the hair on his chest. She snuggled against him, feeling incredibly fulfilled. "Eager to, with you. Not with anyone else."

"Better not be with anyone else," he growled.

Those were the last words she heard before exhausted and totally contented sleep claimed her.

The contentment—the joy—survived even their parting two days later. And the promises they made to each other about her return eased the pain of the separation. They had memories to share and a future to look forward to, and nothing could shake that.

Somehow they had managed to set aside his opinion of her work and her reservations about his apparently uncommitted, reclusive lifestyle. She knew the issues were still there, but after what they had shared, nothing seemed insurmountable. She clung to the memories of his embraces, his loving, their sharing of all the wondrous pleasures of country life.

The memories lasted until she crossed the threshold of The Gallery. Her eyes went immediately to the polished rosewood table where she'd left the fawn. And her heart turned to ice. Numbly, she started toward the table. Before she got there she was intercepted by her partner.

"What did you do with it?" she demanded.

"This," he said smugly, handing her an incredible wad of cash.

"What's this?" she asked, looking vaguely at the money in her hand. It seemed to be all hundred-dollar bills.

"Your share of the proceeds from the sale of the fawn."

Carly felt her stomach lurch. Her eyes went again to the spotlighted table that had held her treasure. Maybe it was still there. Maybe all this was a nightmare. Occupying the fawn's space was a hideous piece of art nouveau crystal. "What have you done?" she asked with the fury of a grizzly bear defending its young.

Fred backed away from her nervously and stammered that he'd received an offer he couldn't refuse. "You wouldn't have refused it either. It was fifty thousand dollars, for God's sake. You ought to be thanking me."

"Get it back."

"Carly, don't be ridiculous. We need the money. If it'll make you feel any better, you can have your share in cash and I'll put mine into our general fund. It was your statue, after all."

"It *is* my statue!" Carly exploded. "And you're going to get it back. Now. And if you have to pay more than you sold it for, it'll come out of your pocket. Your own personal pocket. Not The Gallery's."

"Carly, will you please be reasonable . . ."

"You get that carving back!" Without even realizing it, she was advancing on him, brandishing the cash as if it were a weapon.

"Uh . . . it's probably in Kuwait by now," Fred mumbled, backing away from her.

"Kuwait?"

"You know. On the Persian Gulf? One of those oil-rich countries in the Middle East?"

"I know where Kuwait is!" Carly felt tears threatening her and fought them back. Slowly, she sank down on an oak captain's chair. Kuwait? She'd never see the fawn again.

What was she going to tell Brad? How was she going to tell Brad? He'd trusted her, and she'd betrayed him. She remembered what he'd said about never selling his carvings, and wished she were dead.

Chapter Ten

CARLY CLIMBED TOWARD consciousness both reluctantly and willingly. Willingly, because Brad was waking her up with deft and extraordinarily insolent caresses. Reluctantly, because she knew this was her last day with him. Which, in addition to parting, meant that she could no longer put off telling him what had happened to Pan. The time had flown, the few days dashing past at a headlong pace.

After a week in the city, unable to bear the sight of the empty table or her double-dealing partner, she'd fled The Gallery and Fred. She would have left sooner, but had wanted to make sure that Fred did everything possible to get the fawn back.

Fred himself had been so surprised over the venom of her reaction to his deed, that he had failed even to question her on why she had returned from her buying trip empty-handed; he hadn't indulged in one suggestive remark about how she'd spent her time. But despite his apparent contrition, Carly feared that if she left immediately, trusting his promise to do anything possible to retrieve the carving, she would never see it again.

Fred had surprised her, however, with the industry of his search. By the time she left, they had located the buyer in Kuwait and discovered he'd already sold the carving "to a dealer who was passing through."

Fred claimed the situation was hopeless at this juncture. An unnamed dealer who had been "passing through" would be impossible to find. Carly's expression had caused him to shake his head sadly, and persevere. His Ivy League background provided a ready network of international contacts, and Carly was gratified that he soon had all of them working.

She had postponed her trip as long as she could, not wanting to see Brad until she knew how things stood with the fawn. All week she had prayed that they would be able to get it back immediately. She knew now that it could be months, or years, before the fawn was located. She tried not to think of the worst possible ending. There were no words to describe what Pan meant to her, or to describe how Brad was going to take what had happened.

Brad had accepted her unexpectedly early return with unquestioning joy. His warm welcome had engulfed her before she could even begin to explain about Pan. And then it never seemed an appropriate subject to bring up, even though he had frequently asked her what she was upset about. She knew she had been rationalizing and had set her departure as the deadline for telling him. She couldn't go back to the city with the lie still hanging between them.

But right now was obviously not the time to tell him. His fingers pressed against her, and she let her hips rise as she turned toward him. Her eyes still closed, she sought him blindly with her mouth as she slid her hand up his powerful arm. She dug her fingers into the muscles of his shoulder as their tongues played tag. Her nipples just brushed his brawny chest.

"Are you awake?" he demanded.

"I am now," she gasped as he continued to explore her.

"Hah. I thought you were going to sleep all day."

Her hand found him and measured his readiness. "You are definitely awake."

"About time you noticed!"

She opened her eyes and promptly encountered the dashing twinkle in his dark ones. Why, oh why, did she have to be leaving today? And why had she put off telling him about Pan? She turned her thoughts off. "It is not something you can hide, dressed—or rather, undressed—as you are," she pointed out, escaping into the passion he was building in her.

"I wouldn't say you were exactly gussied up," he pointed out dryly.

"Do you always sleep in the nude?"

"Yep. What about you?"

"Never."

"Is that so?" he asked, running his hand down her naked torso.

"You've corrupted me. What are you doing?"

"Corrupting you further. It'll do you good. Now come here," he ordered, cupping her hip with one powerful palm and drawing her against him.

"Yessir," she agreed. "Like this?"

"Closer."

"How's this?"

"A little closer."

"Close—enough—now?" she asked.

"Yep," he answered, rolling her onto her back, his full weight pressing her into the mattress. "Maybe we'd better keep trying, though," he suggested, moving, thrusting.

"I'm willing if you are," she managed to answer as her entire body dissolved in a glittering haze of pleasure.

"Long as I can, I will," he assured her.

"Forever," she said dreamily. "No, forever would never be long enough." Then she couldn't even try to gasp out words anymore, and had to cling to him as the only solid thing left in a universe gone woozy with ecstasy. She dug her nails into his powerful back and strained every muscle in an effort to engulf his entire body with hers.

"God, you're incredible," Brad sighed as he slowly relaxed, returning from his own pulsating peak.

"You're not so bad yourself," Carly purred, snuggling against his comforting bulk.

"Just, not so bad?" he asked in a hurt tone.

"British understatement."

"You're not British."

"What difference does that make?" she asked, nibbling at his shoulder with little kisses. She cocked her head coyly as his lips toyed with her earlobe. "Are you going to do something about the coffee, or should I?"

"You going to make it the same way you did yesterday?"

"Of course."

"In that case, I'll do it," he responded, drawing away from her with obvious reluctance.

"What was wrong with the way I did it?" Carly demanded in mock outrage.

"Nothing, except you forgot to put the coffee in."

Carly lay on her back, hands under her head, and watched him get up. Lord, but he was a gorgeous hunk of a man!

"I wouldn't have if someone hadn't come storming into the kitchen, slung me over his shoulder, and hauled me off to his cave."

"Who was he? I'll murder the bum."

"Don't do that!" Carly protested. "I loved every minute of it!"

"Have you no shame?"

"About as much as you have," she called as he headed down the stairs.

The smell of coffee finally drew her from the comfortable nest of the warm bed. By the time she was finished in the bathroom, the scent of sausage and eggs had been added. She arrived at the table just as Brad was about to bellow for her.

"Perfect timing," she quipped as she slid into her chair.

"Sure was," he agreed. "You missed all the work."

"I can't help it I take longer in the bathroom than you do," she pointed out reasonably as she dug into the mound of scrambled eggs. "Speaking of which, during the Seventy, are there restrooms along the route?"

"No," he said, grinning. "That going to bother you?"

"No. Just thought I'd ask. Good coffee."

"Thanks. I wish you didn't have to go back," he said softly.

"But I do," she sighed, picking at her eggs, suddenly no longer hungry.

"You're welcome to stay."

"I know."

"But you won't."

She shook her head. If only he knew how badly she wanted to! But until Pan was found, she couldn't possibly abandon The Gallery. Even then?... Maybe it was also because she was scared of making a commitment, and scared Brad's to her wouldn't last.

Brad got up from the table and began clearing away the dishes. "How about a long walk this morning?" he suggested.

"I'd like that." It would be a good time to tell him about Pan.

In the kitchen, Brad whirled suddenly, and Carly found herself in his powerful embrace once again. His mouth, ravenous, demanding, found hers. She clutched him, pressing herself against him hard as he bent her ribs, squeezed the air out of her.

"Let's go for that walk, shall we?" she asked when he finally released her.

"Right," he agreed unhappily.

He was so easy to read. He was almost childlike, in some ways. He had the youthful ardor of a teenager at times. It was both flattering and intimidating. With his passions, and his strength, the thought of him angry was terrifying. Well, maybe he'd understand how she'd managed to lose his gift, and not be furious. She knew she was rationalizing again. How could Brad not be mad? She'd told him enough about Fred for Brad to know that she should have foreseen such a possibility. But she hadn't. She'd never dreamed Fred would do such a thing. She knew now that she'd been a fool. The knowledge didn't help any.

Outside, gray clouds scudded overhead, so close they brushed the tops of the hills. More trees had turned. Now the slopes were an eye-dazzling patchwork of scarlets and oranges and yellows, broken here and there by the dark green of pines and hemlocks or the vivid red of oak.

Fingers interlaced, Brad and Carly strolled through the hay fields down the small stream. Leaves were gathered in a backwater. They turned slowly in the current, fragile craft that from time to time escaped the trap and danced and swirled off toward the river.

"Time for a canoe trip today?" Brad ventured.

"How much more of the river is there to explore?" Carly asked, stalling for time to think. Maybe out on the river would be a better place to tell him. No, she wouldn't be able to see his face if they were in a canoe.

"Plenty. And before we do the race, you'll have to know it all."

"Don't worry. I will. But I can't go today."

"Are you sure you have to go back?"

"Yes."

"Why?"

"My poor spider plant will die if I don't get back to it." The attempt at humor fell flat, but to her relief, Brad let the subject of her departure drop. Wordlessly, they climbed through the hay fields toward the woods.

"Penny for your thoughts?" he asked when they stopped to admire the view.

"Oh, I was just thinking that I'm up here on a buying expedition, and I'm going to have to do something about that before I go," Carly said, evading the real issue.

"And here I thought you'd come just to see me," Brad grumbled, half seriously.

"I wish I could have," Carly said feelingly, giving him a quick hug. "But Fred wouldn't have agreed to The Gallery paying my way in that case." Actually, he probably would have agreed to The Gallery financing a pleasure cruise, his response had been so enthusiastic when she'd said she wanted to go out of town for a while. The atmosphere at The Gallery had been decidedly strained during the past week.

"I would have paid your way," Brad said promptly.

"And made me a kept woman?" Carly countered.

"I'd be overjoyed to keep you."

There it was again, that intensity. "The best things in life are free," she said lightly.

"Did I say you were the best thing in life?" he teased.

"Beast," Carly growled. "Now what are you thinking about?" she demanded when she noticed him studying her speculatively.

"I'm trying to decide if there is anything in life even remotely comparable to you."

Carly snuggled against him. Then she sighed. "Anyway, I'll have to come back with something worthwhile from this trip or Fred will have a cow."

"I had no idea he was pregnant. Want to go to Orlo's?"

Carly frowned. "To tell you the truth, the thought of all those bats doesn't do much for me."

"Dead of winter would be a good time to hit him. Bats will be hibernating and the cold will keep the smell down. If you want, we'll save him for some other time. What do you want to do now?"

"I was planning to stop by Millicent's on the way out of town."

"Haven't you mined that lode enough?"

"Are you kidding? I've hardly scratched the surface," she answered.

"You going to leave her a stick of furniture to sit on?"

"Brad," Carly growled ominously.

"Let me guess. She's probably seventy years old," he continued, "living on Social Security, while inflation eats her alive. And here comes Carly, the white knight, riding gloriously to the rescue, wads of twenties and fifties in hand..."

"Actually," Carly interrupted, infuriated by his willing-ness to jump to totally erroneous conclusions, "she is in her twenties, has two toddlers to feed, and no husband to help."

"All the better," Brad retorted. "An easier target. Can't let the kiddies starve."

"Dammit, Brad!"

"It's business, after all," he observed sourly. "Profit and loss and all that."

"Yes, it is business," Carly agreed angrily, stopping in the middle of the path and turning on him. "It's what makes the world go around."

"I thought that was love," he retorted wryly.

Carly took a deep breath. "Strangely enough, Brad, even people in love have to eat. And to eat, they have to have money. You damn elite idealists, born with silver spoons in your mouths, never seem to realize that. Because you don't know what it's like to go hungry."

"Now wait a minute..."

"No, you wait a minute! Whether you like it or not, I have a job to do." She wondered if she was overreacting because of worrying about Brad's reaction to the news about the fawn.

"Why?"

"What?" Carly asked, caught off stride by the unexpected question.

"Chuck your job. Tell Fred to go pound sand, and get the heck out of that rat race. You don't need it."

"This may come as a bit of a surprise to you, but it so happens that I like my job," Carly said hotly, still wondering why she was reacting this way. "I like my work, and I like living in the city."

"You seem happy enough to come up here to see me."

"I'm beginning to wonder why," Carly fired back quickly.

"I thought it was because you couldn't stay away from me," he answered with a smile.

Carly felt her face get hot. "Oh boy. God's gift to women.

Why was I fool enough to think that Yale had cornered the market on arrogance?"

Brad sobered. "That was a joke? Ha ha?"

"Ha," Carly countered unhumorously, reluctantly letting him draw her close. For a few minutes they walked on, his arm around her easing her misgivings.

"You will admit, though, that you are taking advantage of this woman's circumstances."

"I am doing nothing of the sort," Carly snapped. "And I'd rather not talk about it. It's obvious you still have the same bull-headed prejudice you've always had. It's too bad you didn't take one of those high-falutin jobs you were allegedly so marvelously qualified for. It would have been quite an education for you, living in the real world."

"And this isn't the real world?" he asked, waving his arm at the hillside as they emerged from the woods and headed back down the hill toward the house.

"What was the name of that place in *Lost Horizon*? Shangri-La? This is Shangri-La, cut off from the outside world by the snow-capped peaks of your upper-crust, arrogant Ivy League ignorance."

"This is Ivy League?"

"Wake up and smell the coffee, buster. There's a real world beyond these peaceful hills. It's a world where people have to work hard at jobs they don't like so they can feed their children."

"I know that," Brad protested. "But you just said . . ."

"I said I liked my job, and I do," Carly insisted. "I've been lucky, and I know it. Other people aren't as fortunate, but at least I'm willing to admit it. I'm not so sure your high-flying idealism stands up to too close a scrutiny."

"How's that again?"

"It seems to me that maybe you ran away from the real world," Carly said thoughtfully, looking up at him. "All that stuff about not being an organization man and everything was so much window dressing. I think maybe you were escaping your responsibilities when you came up here."

"Oh?"

"You once made some snide crack about Princeton in the nation's service."

"What's that got to do with anything?"

"I'll tell you what it's got to do with anything. Don't you think you owe the world something for the opportunities you've been given? Don't you think you should be doing something meaningful with all that high-powered learning you acquired?"

"Oh. We're back to the meaningless nature of the work I do," Brad retorted sourly. "Canoes."

"Yes, canoes," Carly agreed. "And your whole life. You're nothing but a carbuncle on the body politic, goofing off up here in the boonies while the rest of the world goes to hell in a handbasket."

"And my carvings..."

"Your carvings are your business. I'm not going to try to change your mind on that. But I would like to point out that at least they would give someone pleasure."

"They do give someone pleasure," he pointed out as they recrossed the little stream. "Me, when I carve them. And need I remind you that I don't hoard them? Seems to me you've got one of them."

Carly felt a cold chill. Oh God, how could she tell him?

Brad apparently didn't notice her dismay and plowed on. "And I suppose what you do benefits the world in some wonderful, altruistic way?" he said with heavy skepticism.

"Strange as it may seem to you, I believe it does."

"How?"

"Okay, so it's a business and I'm in it for the profit, to a certain extent. I'm also in it because I enjoy ferreting out old treasures, because I appreciate the workmanship and beauty in what I find. And if I didn't find the things, probably no one would."

"Practically a saint, aren't you?"

She eyed him steadily for a moment, then turned away. "If you'll excuse me, I have work to do."

As she went inside to finish packing and call Millicent, she realized that in the last few minutes the day had lost all of its beauty. When Brad didn't come into the house while she packed, her heart sank even further. She wondered if subconsciously she'd picked a fight with him so she could avoid telling him about Pan. Anybody would agree that during a fight was *not* the time.

When she emerged, Brad was waiting for her, leaning

against the driver's side door of her car, his arms folded. When she reached for the door handle, he refused to move. She looked up at him and encountered that obstinate, arrogant confidence of his. He was so self-assured, it was infuriating.

She wondered, too, what he was seeing in her eyes. She wasn't even sure herself what she was feeling. She knew she shouldn't leave without telling him about the fawn, but his complete lack of contrition about the things he'd just said made it impossible. She was not going to grovel. Besides, she had meant a lot of the things she'd said.

She wondered what he saw in her. If he really did think she would cheat someone, why did he have her here? The thought that it might be because he only wanted her body made her feel sick.

"You're wrong, you know," he said softly.

"I hope I am," she said, not flinching from his intense dark eyes. "But it seems to me I have exactly as much right to jump to erroneous conclusions as you do."

"And you intend to take full advantage of that right?"

"You bet I do. Now would you get out of my way, please?"

Brad shook his head. "Not likely."

"Now, wait a minute! You can't force me to stay here!"

"No," he assured her. "But I am not about to let you risk your lovely neck in this wreck of a car."

"It seems to me . . ." Carly began, only to be cut off when Brad effortlessly gathered her in. His mouth found hers. In fractions of a second the strength drained out of her resistance and she responded to his kiss. Curling her arms around his brawny torso, she bowed her body to fit it against his.

It was so good in his arms. There was strength and security. There was warmth, and forgetfulness to sand off the rough, cutting edges of the angry words they'd exchanged. She wished it could last forever.

"It seems to me," Brad said after breaking the kiss, "that you could use a porter and a chauffeur. To say nothing of a car that isn't a threat to everyone on the road."

Carly clung to him, trying to get the strength back in her legs. "As for the car, it's not in as bad shape as it looks, and as for the other, I was planning on heading out of here right from Millicent's."

"I figured that out already," Brad said, waving casually at the suitcase she'd dropped in the dirt when he'd grabbed her.

"My, isn't it amazing what four years of college will do for you," Carly retorted.

"I was offering to come along and help."

"All the way to Manhattan?"

"Sure, why not?" he asked with that rakish smile of his.

Carly felt her insides lurch at the thought. Just the prospect of a few more precious hours with him was enough to make her heart sing. Then she realized that if he came to the city, there was no way she could avoid telling him about the fawn. She could hardly ask him to drop her on her doorstep and not invite him up to her apartment. Where he would expect to see his creation. She suddenly decided it would be better for Pan's loss not to come up. He might be located any day now, after all.

"I don't think that's a good idea," she responded carefully.

"Why not? You trying to hide something from me down there?"

"Hide something?" Carly asked guiltily.

"A husband? Six kids?"

"Oh," she answered with relief. "No, of course not. But I have to get the rental car back and everything," she finished lamely.

"You can turn the car in up here and save yourself some money. Besides, it'd give me a chance to say hello to Pan."

Carly wondered if she was going to faint. Somehow she managed to look up into his deep, dark eyes. The instant she did, she knew it was a mistake. Suddenly, there was suspicion bordering on certainty in them.

"He's all right, isn't he?"

"I . . ." Carly stammered.

"What happened to him?" Brad asked, his hands clamping down on her shoulders.

Carly wondered if she had the look of a small, helpless animal caught in a cruel trap. She certainly felt like one. She tried to remember all the ways she'd thought of to tell

Brad, but perversely, her mind was completely blank.
"I . . . don't have him anymore," she said finally.

"WHY?"

"He was at The Gallery . . ."

"YOU SOLD HIM?" Brad literally lifted her off her feet,
then slammed her back down with an abruptness that made
her eyes blur. Or was that from tears?

Carly tried desperately to remember all the answers she'd
worked out in the past week. Her mind remained blank.

"How could you? You . . . I can't believe you!"

"Brad, please! I can explain," Carly protested desperately, reaching for him.

"Forget it! Judas Priest! Profit!" he spat out, then added
an obscenity. "And I was fool enough to think that you were
different. Why are you really here? Hoping to get another
of my carvings out of me by sleeping with me?"

"NO! Please! I can explain!"

"I'll just bet you can. But not to me. Forget it, lady.
Save your breath." As Brad turned furiously away from her,
his angrily clenched fist whirled past her. If she had been
six inches closer, it would have broken her arm.

"Brad?" Carly pleaded as he stalked toward the barn.

"GO TO HELL!" he exploded as he stormed off. "And
take your damn mercenary philosophy and your crummy
rented cars and your Yalie partner with you!"

"Brad, you don't . . . understand," Carly said, her voice
trailing off as he slammed the door of the showroom behind
him.

She slumped wearily against the car. She stood there a
long, long time, hoping desperately that he would come out.
Finally, miserably, she realized that he wasn't going to, and
got in the car. Her hands shaking, she managed to get
it started and headed slowly down his drive. She didn't dare
glance in the rearview mirror. She couldn't bear knowing
he hadn't even noticed she'd left.

Chapter Eleven

THE COLD, GRAY March rain that had somehow managed to trickle its way down inside her slicker had done nothing for Carly's already bleak mood. Wearily, she closed the door behind her and tossed the mail on the spindly little table she'd rescued from a curbside trash heap a month before. Leaning against the wall, she fought her boots off and set them on the boot dryer. Shedding her hooded yellow raincoat, she draped it over a hanger and hung it from the shower curtain rod to dry.

Back in the hall, she studied the small box on the top of the pile of junk mail curiously. It looked like a free sample or coupon offer, but she didn't recall sending for anything since she'd eaten enough cereal to get a Rubik's Cube. That infuriating little gizmo rested in scrambled superiority beside the telephone, something to pass the time spent on hold.

Dropping down on the convertible sofa, Carly lifted her feet to the coffee table where Pan had once resided. She managed to squelch the pang she felt whenever she even looked at the naked spot. In spite of all of Fred's high-powered contacts, it looked as if Pan was gone forever. They had traced the carving to Yemen, then to Saudi Arabia, and finally to Tokyo, where they had hit what seemed to be a dead end. And at every step of the way the price for the carving had escalated, until Carly saw no possibility they could afford to buy it back even if it was located.

Curiously, she shook the box and tried to read the post-mark. There was no return address. The way the stamps had been cancelled was no help. Binghamton, New York, meant nothing to her, except that it was up in Brad's direction.

Wearily, she dropped her head back on the sofa. Wasn't there anything in the world that didn't remind her of Brad? It had been five drab months since they'd argued and split up. She'd heard nothing from him. She had never quite gotten her courage screwed up high enough to actually succeed in reaching him. She'd tried writing to him, but the words had never come. The scraps of paper had formed drifts around her as she'd discarded them.

She'd prayed to hear from him. For weeks after that final, bitter scene she'd waited eagerly for the mail and leaped every time the phone rang. But as the weeks dragged into months, her hopes had faded. It had been the loneliest, saddest Christmas she'd ever known, and now Easter was looming just as depressingly. No rebirth for her this year.

She shook the box. Nothing. It was light, about two inches thick and three inches square. The postman had crumpled two corners slightly to make it fit her mailbox. She'd thought for a minute she was going to have to get a prybar from the building super to get it out.

She picked at the tape with her nail. It was probably plastic salt and pepper shakers allegedly made by starving Indians in the desert Southwest. Finally she got up and liberated a paring knife from the jumble of silverware in the dish drainer.

Leaning forward over the coffee table, Carly slit the tape and found herself facing a wad of tissue paper. Gently, she lifted it out, feeling a sudden tingle of anticipation she didn't dare put a name to.

The entire apartment was suddenly brighter, as if the monarch butterfly she'd just unwrapped had brought with it crisp country air and bright sun to drive back the gloomy city drizzle. Clinging to a bit of bark, Brad's masterpiece looked ready to take flight. Carly set it down on the table before her shaking hands could drop it.

Afraid of its apparent fragility, Carly bent over to study it carefully. The wings were made of the light, translucent plastic Brad used for his canoes. He'd hand-painted them, creating the stained-glass window effect of a real monarch butterfly. The body was incredibly lifelike. The head had bulging, many-faceted eyes. The graceful antennae quivered just from her breathing on them. And the legs, the feet, ended in tiny hooks.

Holding her breath, Carly gently loosened the butterfly from the bit of bark. It was more than just a curio, she realized suddenly. It was the pin she had suggested during that walk in the woods so long ago. The thin, springy wire legs clung to her finger, just as the real butterfly's had clung to Brad's before he'd sent it on its way.

Scrambling to her feet, Carly went to the mirror. A touch, and the butterfly stuck to her sweater, warm, vibrant orange against the green of her pullover. It made her complexion glow and brought out the highlights of her rich auburn hair.

Whirling, then guiltily checking that the butterfly was all right, Carly reached for the box and the wrappings, searching for a note, a message—anything. She wound up throwing the tissue paper around in frustration, leaving it strewn about like snow. The box was no help, either. There was absolutely nothing.

Brad's incomparable talent made her positive that it was his work. That, and, from their walk in his woods, the precious memory shared only by the two of them. She looked down at the butterfly again and seemed to see behind it Brad's face, the way he had looked as he had studied the real butterfly resting so trustingly on his big, powerful finger. She remembered how reverently he had handled that tiny fragment of life, that incredible bit of nature's glory.

Tears stung her eyes at the memory.

With that between them, how could he think she'd deliberately sell Pan? For that matter, Carly mused bitterly as she sank down on the sofa, how could she have said the things to him, about him, that she had? Who was she to criticize him for the way he lived? What right did she have to accuse him of evading responsibility?

Why had he sent this? She touched the butterfly gently, more confident now of its strength. Brad built well. She knew that. He was a master craftsman who put his integrity on the line in everything he did.

She reached for the phone. Her fingers shook as she dialed the 607 area code and then his well-remembered number. She had done this countless times in the last months but had always stopped short, never completed the call. This time she waited, listening to the electronic sounds of the call going through.

Even the ring of his phone was distinctive. Instead of the smooth, sophisticated burr of a city ring, his was harsh and rural.

"Weston speaking."

She nearly fainted at the sound of his voice. "Brad? It's Carly—Carly Meadows," she said huskily, tightening her sweaty grip on the receiver. For an agonizing moment there was silence and she was terrified he was going to hang up on her. When he did speak, it was short and to the point.

"There's a bus, Adirondack Trailways, leaving the Port Authority terminal in an hour. They're holding a ticket for you at the counter." He sounded totally confident.

"A bus?"

"I don't want you driving up here this time of year. The weather's too tricky, especially for the cars you rent."

"But . . ."

"I'll meet you at the bus station in Oneonta."

There was a decisive click, and in a moment she heard the dial tone. "I'll be there," she whispered, acknowledging to herself that not only was resistance useless, but that there wasn't an ounce of it in her entire body.

Her ears still ringing from the brief talk with Brad, she dialed Fred's number.

"I'm leaving for Otego in an hour," she announced when Fred answered.

"To see Brad?"

"He just called. I mean, I called him. He sent me . . . a present."

"How long will you be gone?"

"I don't know."

"Okay. Don't worry about it. I hope things work out."

"Thank you." Much to her surprise, once he understood how much Brad meant to her, Fred had been amazingly sympathetic and supportive. It seemed that his regret over selling the fawn was genuine.

She packed as if she were in a dream. She didn't even change, keeping on the green pullover and white blouse and dark green slacks she'd worn to work. As always, she wore the elk's tooth. Afraid the butterfly might get crushed by her raincoat, she gently freed him from her sweater and shifted him to her hair. He was fashioned perfectly to cling to her rich tresses. She took an umbrella so she wouldn't need to pull her hood over him.

Out on the street, she headed toward Central Park West,

trying to remember what she'd packed, wondering what she'd forgotten, her suitcase feeling treacherously light in her hand. The rain rattled on her umbrella, and cars hissed past, scattering spray as they banged in and out of potholes. Their lights gleamed murkily in the gathering dusk.

For a change, the subway crowding didn't bother her. One of the good things about her apartment and The Gallery was their proximity, which meant she could walk to work. She sometimes wondered if she had a touch of claustrophobia. She avoided buses and subways—especially at rush hour—if she possibly could. But right now she felt as if she were anesthetized.

She flowed with the horde through the underground passage at the 42nd Street IND stop. Ignoring the nun raising funds at the entrance to the bus terminal, the hustlers and vagabonds offering to carry her suitcase, she quickly found the ticket counter. In minutes she was standing at the gate, aware only of the racing of her heart and the stench of bus fumes around her.

Night had fallen by the time they emerged from the slow-moving clog in the Lincoln Tunnel. The New York skyline was shrouded in rain and fog, the towers of the World Trade Center indistinct in the gloomy haze. In impatient lurches, the bus driver determinedly maneuvered his cumbersome charge through the heavy evening traffic.

The ride was interminable. Thanks to a schedule posted by the gate, Carly knew the ride only took four hours. It was the longest four hours she had ever endured in her life. The route took them through the heart of the mountains, on twisting, narrow roads, and they stopped at every minuscule village in the Catskills.

Time and again, Carly was positive they were going to plunge off a cliff and was furious, because now she had something to live for. She tried to doze, but the bouncing, jolting, swerving ride made it impossible. Instead, she spent eternity staring out into the darkness.

Finally Oneonta emerged from the gloom, an oasis of light. Carly grabbed her suitcase and purse and made her way to the front of the bus, gripping seat backs to steady herself. The driver frowned at her, but didn't insist she sit down. She felt her insides twisting tighter and tighter as the bus threaded its way along the back streets to the modern but already worn bus station. They jerked to a halt, the bus rocking on its springs, the air gusting from the brakes with a rude whoosh. The door opened with a wheeze.

Brad was waiting for her. She didn't even touch the ground, simply fell into his arms, crushing herself against him, burying herself in awareness of him—his strength, his scent, his warmth, the rasp of his whiskers against her cheek. He held her suspended, suspended in time and space, swaddled in a cocoon of security and power.

She didn't touch ground again until she stepped from his car. Throughout the half-hour drive neither of them had spoken—Carly, because she was afraid if she did it might shatter what seemed like a dream. Instead, she'd concentrated on soaking up all the joyous sensations of being back here with him.

Once in the house, he carried her up the flight of stairs in the silo, across the living room, and up to the loft. Neither spoke. There was no need. They communicated on a deeper level, expressing needs that used not words, but caresses, looks, and kisses.

His fingers gently touched the butterfly that nestled in her hair, and then he slid his hands down to ease her sweater up. Lifting her arms, she let him draw it off over her head, and then began unbuttoning his shirt as he began unbuttoning her blouse. In a few seconds she was brushing her fingertips over his hairy, brawny chest and he was cupping her breasts, his thumbs toying with her nipples, sending delectable flickers of electricity flashing through her.

He knelt down before her, his hands easing slacks and panties down at the same time. He leaned forward, and his lips found her and he buried his face in her femininity, while she tangled her fingers in his hair and gasped with pleasure. She was shuddering, teetering precariously, by the time he freed her from shoes and slacks and panties and stood up.

Carly fumbled with his belt and then sank to her knees in front of him. She ran his zipper down, unfastened the button of his jeans, drew his clothing down around his ankles. Then she treated him to the same intimate salute of welcome he had just given her. His hand touched her head in what felt like a caress of benediction.

He sank back to sit on the bed, and she continued her worship of him as she worked his feet free. She didn't abandon her post until he insisted, lifting her up to sit astride his lap. He shifted her, steadied her, and they were joined. Their mouths met as he leaned slowly back, pulling her with him.

Thought was impossible in the swirling clouds of ecstasy that engulfed her. She was borne away to paradise with him. Their pleasure peaked simultaneously, and for a long time they just held on, to each other, and to the joy they found in each other. From there, still holding Brad tight, it was a long, smooth slide into secure, dreamlessly deep slumber.

When she awoke, it was to the scent of coffee perking and the warm sunlight in Brad's sleeping loft. There was a faint, pungent smell of wood smoke mingling with the coffee aroma. Sometime during the night he had eased her under the covers. She had no memory of it. She felt totally, bonelessly relaxed, at peace in a way she hadn't been in months—not since she had lain here so long ago.

Her eyes sought out and found the carving of the horned owl overhead. His eyes were very big, very knowing, as he gazed down on the scene of her debauchery, and she wondered if maybe she had gone mad.

"Good morning," Brad greeted her as his head appeared over the edge of the stairs. Then the rest of his magnificent frame rose into view, and Carly was surprised at her disappointment when she saw he was wearing a robe. When had she shed the last vestiges of modesty? Even when she'd modeled, she'd retained them, swaddling herself in detachment, at least, as she'd posed. This man, it seemed, was stripping her of the last shreds of civilization.

Their bodies kept no secrets from each other. But, she wondered, what of their minds? Could they ever reach the same level of sharing and understanding mentally that they had physically? And what of the fawn? Did this mean he had forgiven her?

"Good morning," she answered timidly, easing up in bed, poking pillows behind her back, drawing the sheet up to cover her breasts. Now was the time for words, and she didn't know what to say. Apparently, judging by his silence, neither did he.

"I've got something to show you after breakfast," he

finally announced awkwardly as he handed her a steaming mug.

Carly felt the caffeine streaming through her system from her first sip of his delicious coffee. She wondered if there was anything he didn't do well. "Breakfast," she repeated wonderingly, her stomach suddenly telling her in no uncertain terms that something more than coffee was needed.

"What would you like?" he asked, sitting down next to her.

"The fatted calf?"

"The whole thing?" he responded with that lovely grin of his.

"Yes. I missed supper last night."

"The fatted calf it is," he agreed, getting to his feet and heading for the stairs.

"Brad . . ."

"Eat first," he ordered. "Talk later."

He held her to it, and they ate in silence.

"I'm glad you came," he began as he mopped up the last of his egg with a piece of toast.

"Did I have a choice?"

"I was hoping you didn't. Did you?" he asked, grinning.

"Don't be nosy. Why did you pick that rather unique way of issuing your summons?"

"I was afraid if I asked, I'd say the wrong thing and you wouldn't come. Or that The Gallery still came ahead of me."

"The Gallery never has come ahead of you," she protested.

"Oh?" he asked, skeptically.

"If you're thinking about the fawn . . ."

"I do not wish to discuss the fawn," he interrupted grimly in a tone that brooked no argument.

"What was it you wanted to show me?" Carly asked. She had the feeling they were both being very careful how they handled each other. Outside the bedroom, she amended mentally.

"Down here," he directed, leading the way to the stairs, guiding her to the ground-floor workroom.

"What's that?" Carly asked, staring at the long, lean canoe he was proudly showing her.

"Haven't you ever seen a canoe before?" he teased.

"Canoe, shmanoe," she growled. "Give!"

"It's our canoe for the General Clinton Regatta."

"*Our* canoe? What was wrong with the one we used before?" She didn't even try to analyze her surprise that he was still planning on racing with her and obviously had been for some time. Canoes aren't built in a day.

"That one was designed for two men. This one's balanced for a mixed team. Us, specifically."

Carly moved closer. As did everything he created, the canoe exhibited his meticulous craftsmanship. There was a graceful beauty to its sleek, utilitarian lines. "What's the difference?"

"You weigh about one ten, I figure, while I tip the scales at one ninety, right?"

"Right for me, I don't know about you."

"So if this thing is going to trim right and not fill with water the first time we hit a wave, it's got to balance," he went on. "Which means get the bow up and the stern down."

"Sounds reasonable."

He ran his hand along the smooth hull. "I broadened the beam near the stern, so your seat could be set further back. Then I reshaped the bow so it'll cut the water more efficiently. I could do that because my seat had to be moved back. Now the center of gravity's right."

"You actually went to all this trouble—built a canoe especially for the two of us—when you didn't even know if we were going to see each other again?"

"I knew we would . . ."

"After—the things we said to each other? After what you thought I did?" Carly interrupted awkwardly.

Brad's dark eyes had that burning intensity again. "Those were only words. As for what you did, I told you . . ."

"Words can hurt."

"They certainly can. But what we have surpasses any words we may exchange."

Would he never allow her to explain? Carly let him draw her into his comforting embrace. "I wish I agreed with you," she whispered into his chest, the drumbeat of his heart loud in her ear. "I wish I believed you." His arms around her, warm as they were, couldn't thaw the icy lump of fear in her chest. He kept his arm around her as he guided her upstairs and they settled together on the sofa. Outside, the world was gray and bleak, but Carly thought it was the most beautiful sight she'd ever seen.

"You just never quit, do you," she purred as he slid his hand under her sweater.

"Not when you're around, I don't," he agreed, his lips brushing her hair as, working blind, he skillfully unbuttoned her blouse.

"Sir! What are you doing?" Carly gasped as he probed past her bra.

"Seducing you."

"Oh. Just checking. Don't stop."

He stopped. "Was that 'Don't, period, stop, period'? Or was it 'Don't stop, period'?"

Carly slid her hand up and curled her fingers around the back of his neck, drawing his mouth down toward hers. "It was 'Don't stop, exclamation point,' you beast." She fastened her mouth to his and attacked. Her other hand slid to his lap.

"It is impossible to keep my hands off you," Brad murmured hoarsely a moment later as he wrestled with her clothes. Carly lifted her hips so he could shove her pants down and concentrated on reaching only the most important part of his.

In a few minutes, she was straddling his lap, savoring fullness once again. She linked her hands behind Brad's neck and leaned away so she could look deep into his dark eyes.

"Better move this guy," Brad noted, gently detaching the butterfly.

"We could hook him in this rug of yours," Carly pointed out, unbuttoning his plaid shirt to bare his hairy torso.

"Is that a comment on the hirsute state of my chest?" he asked as he liberated Carly's sweater, then shoved her shirt back off her shoulders.

"I love the hirsute state of your chest," Carly purred, twisting one of the black strands around her finger.

"Good thing, because I'm not about to take up shaving there." His hands slid from her breasts around to her back, then down to her waist. "God, I love you!"

Carly shivered. "Is that your glands talking?"

Brad grinned. "Just what do you think is in control right now?"

"Your id," Carly said, sighing. "And id's a good thing, too."

"You got a code in your head?" Brad joked back shakily as she moved, swinging her hips in a primitively wanton circle.

"Mmmm," Carly sighed as the sensations raging through her made it harder and harder to talk. His hands were tight and strong as they gripped her waist, helping her move. His thumbs dug into her soft belly, slid lower, and pressed. She threw her head back and inhaled convulsively as ecstasy blistered her.

Reaching down, she found him and heard him groan at her feathery touch. Then she was cresting, and she felt him joining her in a soaring fountain of pleasure. Later, she slowly leaned forward to stretch out along him as he lay back against the sofa.

Eventually, he slid sideways, drawing her with him so they were on their sides. She could feel the warmth of the fire on the backs of her bare legs.

She nuzzled his cheek contentedly and snuggled into his comforting embrace. But there was a serpent in their paradise. She knew, as long as it remained unresolved, their future was marked for disaster. How could she explain what had happened? And would he believe her?

Chapter Twelve

PAINFULLY AWARE OF how cold the water would be in the middle of May, Carly tried to steady the canoe. Mercifully, there was no wind. Otsego Lake was flat and oily-looking under an ominously hazy gray sky. Ahead, to her right, a quarter of a mile away, she could see Cooperstown and the dock she and Brad had shoved off from fifteen minutes before. Around them, twenty or thirty other canoes jostled for position along the invisible starting line between a red float and the small powerboat.

"I had no idea there were this many nuts in the world," she observed nervously.

Brad laughed from his place in the bow. "Wait till you see the start of the Seventy. There'll be a couple of hundred canoes out here."

"You realize of course that this entire expedition is insane." She was trying not to think of the thirty-five miles of hard paddling that lay ahead of them. The Little Red Caboose Race was billed as a warm-up for the General Clinton Regatta at the end of the month. Carly had the feeling today was to be her baptism of fire, as well as a good indication of whether she could make the Seventy. She'd had remarkably little time to train.

"Nervous?" Brad asked, turning to glance over his shoulder at her.

"Nervous? Me? Never! Terrified, yes. Nervous, never!"

"Good, the adrenaline will do you good."

"So much for sympathy," Carly sighed, resting her paddle across her legs, keeping a hand on it while she adjusted her life jacket. She noticed that most of the competitors weren't wearing any. She felt a little self-conscious in the bulky yellow vest, but a lot more secure and definitely warmer.

"Sympathy comes with the chicken barbecue you get when we finish." He started to say something else, but was interrupted by a squeal of feedback as someone turned on the portable PA system in the powerboat.

"Okay, a couple of special announcements before we get underway," the race official began. "The river's unusually high, so you'll have to watch for a few things. As you pass behind Bassett Hospital, there's a wire across the river. Keep to the left and be ready to duck.

"Second thing is the low bridge on the Clark estate. Yesterday you couldn't make it under it. But it should be possible to slip through today. If not, you'll have to portage around it on the right. Any questions? Okay, we start in thirty seconds. Let's straighten up that line out there, and you turkeys at the far end quit trying to creep ahead."

"I wish we'd practiced this stretch of the river," Carly said nervously.

"Not my fault you didn't get up here more often."

"Please, let's not go into that now," Carly pleaded. She felt shaky enough about the race without adding another argument with Brad. The strain between them had been building steadily as The Gallery had interfered with their practice schedule.

The search for the fawn continued. Carly refused to let discouragement overwhelm her. She drove the increasingly reluctant Fred on mercilessly, until he was afraid his old school ties would disown him.

Carly had considered telling Brad of the attempts to get Pan back, but the possibility of them ever actually coming to anything seemed so remote that she'd decided not to say anything. Pan was always intruding on her thoughts and, she was certain, Brad's, too. It was like a pebble in her shoe. She held her paddle ready as the starter called the racers to their marks.

The flat crack of the starting gun echoed out across the lake and was quickly replaced by the sound of churning water. There was the thump and thud of paddles hitting paddles and the sides of canoes as the boats jostled for position.

Brad had placed them on the far right end of the starting line. Carly glanced to her left and was relieved to see that they were holding their own—so far, at least. She barked a sharp "hut," and switched to the other side, pleased at the quickness with which she could do it. She'd felt a bit of a fool standing in the middle of her living room practicing it, but it looked like it was going to pay off.

Brad had his head down, his entire body swinging as he put his back into his paddling. He had a long piece of plastic tubing from an insulated jug of Gatorade clamped between his teeth. Carly's tube was within easy reach of her mouth, snapped to her vest with a clothespin. Her jug and a spare paddle were taped to the thwart ahead of her. Beside her, in a plastic bucket, was a small bunch of bananas.

Carly glanced at the mass of canoes to her left and saw that some of them were pulling ahead, so she increased the power of her strokes, pulling harder, but still carefully keeping in sync with Brad. She was counting to herself, trying to estimate how they were doing. She knew at this point Brad wanted a pace of about seventy strokes a minute.

The ragged line of canoes began to funnel into the narrow end of the lake, bunching up, banging against each other as they fought for position in the headwaters of the Susquehanna. On the map, this part looked like a misshapen tadpole, the fat body pinching off into a long, skinny, twisting tail. Posh houses dominated the shoreline. A sparse but enthusiastic crowd lined the low banks, cheering, calling encouragement to their friends or favorites. There was another gathering on the first bridge, a hundred yards or so from the lake. Carly saw Joe Johnson, Brad's amputee buddy, yelling at them, but couldn't hear what he was saying.

As soon as they were past the bridge, they kept to the left, heading for the willow tree that marked the start of the first portage. Carly could hear the water rushing over the small dam that backed up Otsego Lake. She kept pulling for all she was worth, knowing that getting to the portage as soon as possible would give them an advantage, then ruddered to keep from hitting the rotting pilings at the landing. The canoe ahead of them was yanked out just in time. Brad leaped into the knee-deep water. Carly stowed her paddle and followed, sucking in a surprised breath at the chill.

She scrambled up the bank and gave a heave as Brad hoisted the canoe up onto his shoulder. He set off at a run, almost yanking the canoe out of her hands. Staggering across the road, Carly nearly fell as she scrambled over the guard rail on the other side. From there they plunged down the steep incline.

"How you doing?" Brad asked, not even panting as they launched the canoe in the boiling current.

"Great," Carly gasped, getting in, tripping over her paddle because she'd left it on the wrong side. "Let's go!"

"Remember, to the left," Brad reminded her. "I'll steer."

"Right," Carly agreed, wondering for the hundredth time since the start why in the world she'd gotten herself into this. It was absolutely mad. She tried not to think about the thirty-five miles of river looming ahead of them like a serpentine monster.

Kinky madness here, on the upper stretch. Barely twelve or fifteen feet wide in most places, the river twisted and turned, constantly looping back on itself. The current was swift but not choppy, driving them along steadily. Brad called the switches here, as they'd agreed, barking them back over his shoulder without ever missing a beat.

They came to the wire and sailed under it with room to spare. If they'd been six feet to the right, it would have caught him in the throat.

Whenever the river bent abruptly, Carly noticed, he'd plan ahead so she would be paddling on the outside of the curve. He sometimes paddled on the same side she did, or if it was really tight, bow-ruddered them around the bend, jamming the blade of his paddle into the water so the canoe pivoted sharply around it.

Other canoes surrounded them, a few ahead, many more behind, judging by the sounds of paddles and paddlers. Carly watched the bow of an opponent creep up on them. She dug in harder, and seeing it slide back out of sight, felt a surge of pride. Ahead, two canoes tangled, and she and Brad gained on them. Brad started past them on the left, then braked sharply and cut back the other way as the tangle twisted sideways in the current. Just as she and Brad sprinted past, one of the canoes tipped, dumping the cursing team in the cold water.

In the clear for a minute and able to relax a little, Carly began to be aware of a growing ache in her shoulders. She changed her stroke and tried to ignore the pain as Brad called another switch. How far had they come so far? A mile, maybe? God, how was she ever going to make it? Remembering what Brad had drilled into her, she pushed away all thought of the future and concentrated on the present.

As the crowding diminished, she began to enjoy the scenery more. They entered a stretch that looked like something out of Longfellow's *Hiawatha*. Gloomy hemlocks leaned out over the water on both sides. The river ran deep and swift here, and there was an eerie mist rising from the surface. The thick trees soaked up the sound of their paddling, and Brad's voice was reverently hushed as he called, "Hut." Now she knew that today wasn't a mistake. She would remember this forever—being on the river with Brad, pitting themselves against nature and their own human frailty, to say nothing of thirty other canoes.

The river opened out again, the hemlocks falling behind to be replaced by gnarled pin oaks and straggly willows. All along the bank, trees had been undermined by the current. In some places they clung to the shore with twisted, scarred roots. Beneath were mysterious dark holes fit for trolls. Some trees had lost the battle, had toppled in to block the channel. So far, there had always been space to make it through without portaging. In a few places, someone had obviously been at work with a chain saw.

At one point Carly was sure Brad had made a mistake. He cut them sharply to the left, but the main channel obviously went to the right. She was about to say something when they ducked into a narrow, almost invisible chute. She looked back and saw that he had bypassed a large, slow loop half blocked by a fallen tree. Her respect for his knowledge of the river grew even greater.

It was as if they were in a weird fantasy world where nothing existed but them and the misty river, with its high banks lined with weeds and trees. Because of the tight twists and turns, even the other canoes were lost from sight. From time to time she could see beneath the surface the sunken, waterlogged mass of a fallen tree, bare of bark, slowly decaying in the mud.

The current was swift and smooth, driving them along, and Brad eased the pace a little. Around the curves he allowed just enough room between them and the outside bank for paddling. Sometimes he figured it too close, and Carly had to push them away, her blade digging into the soft mud.

They rounded a bend and found themselves bearing down on a very low bridge. Carly assumed Brad would take them to the bank to portage around it. Instead, he set a course straight for it. Her heart rose into her throat. At the last moment, just when she was sure he was going to be decapitated, he dropped flat on his back. She had been so absorbed in worrying about whether he was going to hit it, she barely had time to duck. The steel beam almost smashed her in the face. She had a blurred view of the underside of the bridge speeding past inches from her nose, a kaleidoscope of rusty, stained steel, and then it was gone and she levered herself up and got back to paddling.

Brad glanced over his shoulder at her and grinned. "I figured if I fit under, you would," he called cheerily. Carly smiled wryly back at him.

As more and more tributaries entered the river, it began to widen and go faster. The challenge of staying in the swiftest part of the current, using it to their best advantage, made it possible for Carly to ignore the growing weariness in her arms and shoulders. Also, the aches faded as her muscles warmed and her body began drawing on deeper reserves of energy.

There were few spectators to cheer them on, which wasn't surprising, as most of the route was through either wilderness or tilled fields. From time to time there would be a bridge and a few people yelling encouragement. Carly always flashed them a grin and tried not to feel too thrilled with herself. Brad was doing most of the work, after all.

A large crowd was waiting at a bridge more impressive than the others they'd hit. "Milford," Brad yelled over his shoulder. "Almost halfway."

Halfway! Only halfway? She felt as if she'd been paddling most of her life. Then she remembered she hadn't drunk anything—how could she have forgotten after all Brad's lectures on not getting dehydrated? She groped around, located the straw to her Gatorade, and sucked hard, wondering if it had somehow gotten clogged. Finally, she got it going, and it tasted like ambrosia, making it hard to take only a few sips—she didn't dare drink so much that they'd have to stop.

Halfway. That meant they had seventeen miles of river behind them. How long had they been out? An hour, maybe two? It was a good thing she didn't have a watch. Trying not to think about the remaining eighteen miles, Carly dug in, twisting to put the load on her back instead of her shoulders and arms.

Ahead of her, Brad continued paddling like a machine. His tousled black hair was wet with sweat in spite of the cloudy, cool spring weather. The sleeves of his T-shirt were sodden. The hair on his arms was plastered down by a mixture of sweat and spray.

About a mile farther on, it began to rain. She tipped her head back, let the cool drizzle sprinkle her face for a moment, then blinked to get the water out of her eyes. The surface of the river blossomed into dainty spreading rings of ripples.

The current was gone, and Carly knew they were into the stretch backed up by Goodyear Dam. Brad was guiding them from point to point, cutting off as much of the distance as he could rather than taking the longer, sweeping outside course he'd used where there was current to help them. The river was twenty or thirty yards wide here.

"How you doing back there?" he called around his Gatorade straw.

"Just great," Carly assured him, trying not to pant. Their speed had dropped along with the current and she had the feeling they were barely moving.

"Eat something," he ordered.

"Thanks," Carly said gratefully, slipping her paddle into the bottom of the canoe while he kept up his steady stroking. Reaching down, she grabbed a banana and quickly peeled it. The energy from the rich, sweet fruit seemed to go right to her muscles. In a few moments she had wolfed it down, followed it with a swallow of Gatorade, and resumed paddling. "Your turn," she called.

Brad gave a heartfelt sigh as he set his paddle between his legs, then straightened up and stretched. Careful not to unbalance the canoe, he twisted around and faced her. "How are you doing?"

"Fine." Carly basked in the glow of his approving smile as she kept them moving, flipping her paddle from one side of the canoe to the other to keep them on course.

A long, straight stretch gave her a chance to survey the opposition. The men in the canoe in front of them seemed to be faltering. When Brad finished eating and began paddling again, Carly felt the canoe leap forward under her. Encouraged, she set her sights on catching the pair ahead.

It was obvious from the way Brad was paddling that he had the same idea. Their rivals grew steadily closer. Carly pulled even harder, and they drew even, rounding them on the outside of a sweeping bend, then surging ahead, leaving them behind. The small triumph boosted Carly's spirits.

It seemed like forever before the broad expanse of Goodyear Lake opened out in front of them. Carly tried not to think of the brutal portage that lay at the end of it and used the excuse of bailing some of the water out of the canoe to grab a short rest. It was a standing joke between them that when she got tired, she bailed. It was the first time she'd done it today.

The rain streamed down on them, pounding the water flat, giving it the appearance of hammered metal. It formed strange patterns on the lake surface, created bubbles that winked out of existence a second after they were born. The cold water cascaded down over Carly's face, making her blink to get it out of her eyes. It ran down inside her life jacket in aggravating, tickling rivulets.

Eons of drenching effort later, the line of barrels marking the end of the lake came into view. Much to her surprise, Carly was thrilled by the sight, because it meant a chance to get out of the canoe. Her arms and shoulders had stopped aching, but right now her bottom was killing her. Then, her feet squishing in her sodden sneakers, she looked up at the twenty feet of slippery mud they had to climb and wondered what Brad would say if she announced she wanted to quit.

"Come on, partner," Brad urged, bending to pick up the canoe.

Somehow, Carly managed to shove aside thoughts of quitting. Together with Brad, she gave a heave and a twist and flipped the canoe upside down over her head. Muddy water cascaded down over her. Brad looked around to see why she was cursing and burst out laughing. She was about to put her end down and go punch him one when another canoe pulled in at the landing.

"Let's go, buster," she growled, suddenly eager to be on their way. Maybe she'd have a chance to sock him at the bottom of the hill. The last of her bananas, the only thing not tied to the canoe or held in by the thwarts, wound up trampled into the mud underfoot. Skidding and slipping, she scrambled up the bank. Brad set such a fast pace that she had to trot to keep up. If they'd had the seventy-pound aluminum, she knew she'd never have made it.

It took all of her anger to sustain her on the hair-raising scramble down to the river and not cringe as she studied the current that boiled past. It had to be at least twice as bad as the first time they'd done this stretch, and that had been in the lovely, safe, tough, stable Grumman. By the time they set the canoe down, Carly had completely forgotten she was mad at Brad for laughing at her, and wasn't aware of anything except how tired and cold and sore she was.

"How are you doing?" Brad asked as he eased the canoe into a backwater.

"Tell me again what a great time I'm having," Carly said breathlessly.

Brad guffawed and offered her his hand as she stepped into the canoe. The extra squeeze he gave her as he bent over to kiss her did more for her morale than anything he could have said. She held them steady while Brad scrambled into the bow.

Then they were off and away again, and Carly was too busy and too scared to be tired. All she could think about was that they had to keep going faster than the river. She flipped her paddle from side to side without even thinking about it, somehow knowing what Brad wanted without being able to hear his calls over the roar of the water.

They plunged down the terrifying toboggan ride like a runaway log. Carly's paddle ricocheted off the bottom as she worked desperately. It was more like a controlled crash than anything else, one hair-breadth escape after another, as far as she was concerned. Boulders loomed up ahead of them and then were past, so close she could have reached out and touched them if she'd had the time. More than once the canoe scraped through with a nasty grating sound.

They raced under a bridge, and Carly was ready when
Brad dug his paddle in, cutting them hard to the right. On
her left, she saw two teams portaging out of the cul-de-sac
they had gotten caught in and mentally congratulated Brad
for his cleverness.

Something about the mad dash lifted Carly's spirits and
renewed her strength. The adrenaline poured out, refreshed
her, and she paddled harder than ever as the river slowed
once more. Even the rain drenching them could do nothing
to spoil her high.

"Let's make it look good!" Brad called suddenly, and
Carly realized with a surge of pride they were almost there.
Their strokes became crisp and tightly timed as they powered
down on the flat-draped rope that marked the finish.

Carly took one last mighty stroke just before they crossed
the line, then dug her paddle in to rudder them toward the
shore. Slumping with exhaustion, she felt the bow of the
canoe bury itself in the mucky bank.

There was a crowd of people, hauling at her, hauling at
the canoe. Brad's huge hand engulfed hers and, one-armed,
he hoisted her out of the boat. His feet ankle-deep in the
mud, he gathered her to him in a crushing embrace. Carly
held on, afraid if she let go she'd collapse.

Two hours later, she was soaking her weary, aching body
in Brad's monster tub. "I can't believe I did it," she sighed
contentedly between sips of the hot toddy Brad had fixed
for her.

"Ninth," Brad grunted as he lounged beside her.

"Are you disappointed?" she asked worriedly.

"Are you kidding? Ninth out of twenty-seven starters is
terrific for a mixed team, especially considering how little
training time we've had together."

Carly relaxed, letting the penetrating heat of the water
meet the outgoing warmth of the toddy. She was beginning
to think that maybe she would be warm again, after all. She
knew she was going to be hungry again, because she already
was. She had gone through her plate of barbecued chicken,
mashed potatoes, and cole slaw as if she'd just escaped from
a concentration camp, and then tried to con Brad out of
some of his.

The exuberant crowd under the tent had been wet and
sweaty and steamy, reeking of the river and wet clothes.

The temperature had dropped, and rain had streamed off the canvas while a cold wind had whipped misty spray through the tent's interior. Only the press of the crowd had kept them all from freezing.

From time to time the arrival of another canoe was greeted with raucous applause and yelling. Everyone seemed to know someone, and in most cases that someone was Brad. Carly had lost track of the number of times she'd been introduced, how the introductions had been phrased, and knew she'd never remember the names of any of the people she'd met. Joe Johnson had been there, oblivious of the way his prosthetic leg had sunk into the mud. Everyone had been soaked and bedraggled. Some were in expensive rain gear, most just in sodden shorts and T-shirts. More than anything else, the crowd had resembled a gathering of flash flood refugees at a Red Cross tent.

"That was without a doubt the craziest thing I have ever done in my entire life."

"Didn't you like it?" Brad asked anxiously.

"Are you kidding? I loved it!"

"Thank God," he breathed.

"Which only goes to show how crazy I am."

"You think that was crazy, wait until we do the Seventy," he chuckled.

"Is it twice as hard?" she asked, wondering if she could possibly endure twice the agony she had today. Her forearms felt like someone was driving knives into them. If she'd had this much trouble doing thirty-five miles, what on earth made her think she could do seventy?

"No. Physically, it's about the same. Joe put it well—the first half is physical, the second half is mental."

"I feel like I've been mugged by a river," she grumbled.

"I thought you enjoyed it," he responded, obviously still worried.

Carly managed to give him a hug and rested her cheek against his muscular shoulder. "I wouldn't have missed it for anything," she said softly. "It was—I don't know how to put it . . ."

"There's something special about meeting that kind of challenge," Brad finished for her.

"That's part of it. And it probably sounds corny, but I

feel closer to you when we're out on the river than I do at almost any other time."

"Any other time?" he asked, his voice dripping passion.

"I said *almost* any other time," she laughed, giving him another hug. "But I'm not sure I can handle the Seventy."

Brad gently drew her over so she was lying on top of him. He cuddled her reassuringly, his lips nuzzling her hair. "You'll be able to make it," he assured her. "You'll be in better shape by then."

"But it's only two weeks away," she protested.

"Plenty of time if we work at it."

"I hope you're right," she sighed. "I don't suppose I can chicken out at this point, can I?"

"And leave me without a partner? Not on your life! Anyway, I wouldn't want to do it with anyone but you."

"You say the sweetest things."

"White man speak only the truth," Brad said solemnly.

"Like Cochise, I wait ninety days to be glad," Carly answered gravely. She rested her cheek on Brad's hard, hairy chest and listened to the slow, powerful drumming of his heart.

"You won't be disappointed," he replied, his hands cupping her hips gently, lovingly.

"Know what?" she asked after long, delectable minutes in his arms.

"What?"

"I'm falling asleep and I'm hungry."

"So, my dear, am I. If I go slay a brontosaurus, will you cook it?"

"Only if you clean it first," she said, still nestled on top of him as if he were a bed.

"Would you like pancakes?"

"At this hour of the day?"

"So call them crêpe suzettes, or forget what time it is. It's what I can whip up fast, because I've got the mix. And right now we are both suffering from a carbohydrate shortage. Real maple syrup," he added.

"Mmmmm, you talked me into it."

He slid out from under her and climbed out of the tub. "You stay here and relax. I'll call you when things are ready."

From the dinner table, Carly was barely able to make it up to bed. She was delectably aware of Brad's closeness as she slid off into a deep, dreamless sleep.

The closeness lasted until the next day, when she was forced to admit to herself and to him that she had to leave. Always there were partings from Brad. Lord, how she hated to say good-bye.

"You're welcome to stay," Brad noted for the hundredth time. "We've got the Phelps Hose Race, and then the Regatta." She felt he was using the races as a hold on her. He didn't need to do that, he had an emotional grip on her that was unbreakable. But there were things in the city that she couldn't simply ignore.

"I'll be up here for them both," she assured him as she packed. "But I just can't stay here for two weeks . . . The Gallery."

"Damn The Gallery," Brad said impatiently. "Every time I turn around it's the same old thing! Why the hell do you keep using that as a wall between us? I love you."

Carly froze at the statement, suddenly trapped in a whirlpool of emotions.

"Is that your glands talking again?" she asked, trying to make light of his admission while she worked frantically at sorting out her own feelings.

Brad swept her into his crushing embrace. "It's my entire body, my whole being, talking. Stay with me!"

"I wish I could . . ."

"But?"

She shivered. "I've got to get back."

"How can you put The Gallery between us like some damn rival lover?" Brad asked furiously, pushing her away, holding her at arm's length.

"There might be news of Pan," she said desperately, not wanting her visit to end in a fight, forgetting that she had decided not to tell Brad about the recovery efforts. "We're trying our darndest to get him back."

"Noble," he snorted. "I thought I made it clear long ago that I didn't want to talk about Pan. So you made a buck out of him! I can forgive that."

"That's a pretty crummy pun," Carly said bitterly, suddenly furious with Brad for not appreciating the fact that she was doing everything possible to get the fawn back. Or that she hadn't been the one to sell it in the first place. Of course, Brad didn't know that. He was too stubborn to listen. She looked up at him, a lot more bravely than she felt. "It's gracious of you to forgive," she said sarcastically, "but you and I both know you can't forget. Dammit, Brad, you've got to let me explain. Do you think I could stand living with you—being married to you—knowing what you think of me? Because believe me, marriage is part of the deal."

"I never said it wasn't." Brad sighed wearily. "Why do your visits always have to end this way?" he asked softly.

Carly stiffened her resolve. "Maybe it just isn't meant to be for us," she said, with a sadness that burned deep into her soul. She'd tried everything she could think of. What else was there?

"I can't believe that," Brad argued, trying to draw her into his arms.

"I've got to go," Carly announced, evading him.

"We've got races," he noted as he followed her out to her car. "Next weekend, and then the week after that is the regatta."

"I'll be here," Carly assured him, and managed a wan smile. "At least we can have that."

"Are you really that enamored of the city and The Gallery?"

Carly shook her head. "I love it up here. But The Gallery is in the city, and the way things are, if I pull out now, I'll lose my entire investment. I won't do that."

"If it's a matter of money, I could..."

"It's not just the money," Carly argued. "It's pride, too. I can't just chuck it all without a fight. But none of that's really important. As long as you feel, deep down in your heart, the way you do about me, that I'd let Pan be sold so I could make a profit, I can't see how our love could last."

She felt as if she were dying. Apart from this one, basic misunderstanding, they had so much. Everything.

Brad seemed about to argue the point, then stopped himself. "Well, I guess that's that," he agreed softly.

Carly nodded desolately. She tried to think of something to say, of some way to save the situation, but couldn't. Her brain was incapable of coming up with anything new. Because there is nothing new to come up with, she told herself forlornly, miserably.

"One thing I do want, though," he said briskly.

"What?"

"If we're going to have a decent shot at finishing the Seventy, you've got to be up here the entire week beforehand." He opened the car door for her and tossed her suitcase in.

"Why?"

"Training."

Somehow, Carly managed a smile. "Are you sure that's the reason? Or are you planning to try to keep me in bed the whole time?"

"Well," he answered, grinning, "you'll need plenty of rest. But seriously, there are sections of the river we've got to practice together. Especially that section around the trestle. Besides, the last week before the race is crucial in any kind of an endurance event. How about it?"

Carly gnawed her lip. A week with Brad on the river? Talk about paradise. "Okay," she agreed at last.

"And just maybe somewhere along the line we'll succeed in changing things between us," he said softly as he leaned over her car.

"You never give up, do you?" she observed as she put the key in the ignition.

"Endurance racers never give up. Haven't you caught on to that by now?" He leaned in the window and kissed her. "Drive carefully."

Chapter Thirteen

CARLY HAD THE feeling she and Brad were paddling through a misty void. Ahead of them, canoes floated unsupported, like something out of an Ingmar Bergman movie, surreal and obscurely symbolic. Scores of them were suspended on the invisible gray plane of Otsego Lake. The morning fog made the sky and water blend into each other, stealing their horizon.

She had the feeling, too, that she and Brad were paddling into a future just as vague and featureless. Where would they go from here? After this weekend, for the two of them, there was nothing.

For now, the only solid thing was the canoe around her. The only tangible security was her life jacket and the spare paddle taped to the canoe with wide strips of aluminum duct tape. She had the feeling she was about to take a giant step off into emptiness. Seventy miles of river was too much to comprehend. Fifty years of future without Brad was too terrifying to contemplate.

In front of her, as they would be for the next ten hours, were Brad's broad shoulders, the muscles bulging under his T-shirt. He swung the paddle with an easy grace. His curly black hair was misted with fog.

The half-mile-long starting line emerged from the mist. Canoes were strung out across the lake like beads on a loose string, those on the far end shadowy silhouettes, the ghosts of the Iroquois, the shades of the last of the Mohicans. Carly was sure James Fenimore Cooper would have loved it.

Brad steered them toward the line, picking an open space as close to the end as he could. Their plan was to get off the line fast and get into the river with the leaders. With a hundred and twenty canoes trying to fit down the funnel, there were bound to be jams.

As they waited, Carly reached for a banana and peeled it absently. For two days Brád had been stuffing them both with high-calorie foods. Carbo-packing, he called it. She'd eaten enough pasta in the last forty-eight hours to refloat the *Andrea Doria*. The theory was that the body would draw on the stored calories during the ten hours of the race.

No one was talking much. Even Brad was subdued. A few fog-muffled voices discussing last-minute strategy drifted over the lake. It was as if the gravity of what they were all attempting was sinking in. Once in a while there was the nervous laughter of a gladiator about to enter the arena.

The start was unlike anything Carly had ever heard before. It was as if Niagara Falls had suddenly been unleashed, with a ragged drum roll as accompaniment. Paddles tore into the placid lake surface and thundered off the flanks of the canoes. One canoe, unbalanced by the wake of two faster boats, capsized.

The line held and held and held, and then slowly grew ragged, began to fray, like a jet's contrail being torn apart by the wind. Carly pulled harder, matching Brad as he set a brutal pace. She kept the bow of the canoe pointed just to the right of the ancient cannon marking the entrance to the river. Every canoe team, except a few that were having trouble steering, was heading for the same narrow gate. Mercifully, she and Brad were among the first through.

Then they were away from the first portage, plunging down the river. It was gloriously mad chaos! The blood was coursing through Carly's body with all the passion of the hunt. Crowds of people lined every accessible portion of the bank, jammed the bridges over them. She heard people calling to Brad, even heard her name a few times.

The first half of the Seventy duplicated the Little Red Caboose Race, except that with four times as many entrants in their class, the narrow, twisting headwaters were a mob scene. Where snags narrowed the channel, canoes sometimes stacked up like cordwood. Brad would plunge into such jams, showing no quarter as he bulled their way through. This was, he reminded her when she protested, a race.

There was a huge throng at the Milford bridge. Brad angled in toward the left bank, and Carly tried to spot Joe Johnson, who was again acting as their support crew. Joe had driven them up to Cooperstown, in plenty of time for the seven o'clock start, and was following them down the river with jugs of Gatorade and bags of fruit and candy.

Milford, a quarter of the way through the race, was their first supply point.

Carly saw Michelle and Frank, friends of Brad's, but couldn't see Joe anywhere. Then suddenly he appeared and reached out and grabbed their canoe, hauling them to a stop. "How's it going?" he asked as he filled Brad's jug.

"Great," Brad answered. "Except for idiots who can't steer a canoe."

"Are you referring to me?" Carly demanded.

"Of course not. You're doing fine. I'm talking about the jerks who keep getting crosswise. They ought to make the aluminums start after us."

"A fine idea, except then none of them would get there before midnight," Joe noted.

"Really?" Carly asked.

"I'm exaggerating a little. But it does take two or three hours longer in an aluminum." Once again, Carly was glad they weren't in the Grumman.

"Ready to go?" Brad asked, his mouth full of apple.

"Lay on, MacDuff," she called, cramming the last of a banana into her mouth.

"And damned be him that first cries hold! Enough!" Brad responded, driving his paddle in, shooting them back out into the river.

After the early burst of competitive fury, when the river was too narrow for everyone to fit through at once, a camaraderie developed between the contestants. Aside from the pros, who started an hour after the amateurs, shooting past, paddling with grim determination, the grouping of canoes remained relatively constant. As they entered the grueling stretch leading to the Goodyear Dam portage, Carly exchanged cheerful words of encouragement with the other teams.

The river was wide and slow, and even with the aluminum canoes they were overtaking there wasn't the crowding there had been. There was also an unspoken acknowledgment that they were all in this together, that the opponents were now the river and their own exhaustion. The fog burned off completely by the time they were halfway across Goodyear Lake. The sun was hot on Carly's arms and back as she pulled the paddle through the water with monotonous regularity.

When they reached Goodyear Dam, Carly realized for the first time how much better shape she was in than she had been for the Caboose race only two weeks ago. The portage was a quick trot up the slope and down the ravine. She was tired but far from exhausted, drawing on the stamina she'd built up with hundreds of laps in the Y pool and a good many miles on the river.

The radio tower that was the landmark for the finish of the Little Red Caboose Race appeared, and Carly felt a surge of pride. They were halfway, and she was feeling great. They swept past the airpark, invisible except for the familiar muddy bank and a cheering crowd. Carly took a deep breath. They were entering the one stretch of river that was absolutely unforgiving—even the pros avoided it when the water was high. If she and Brad made a mistake here, at the very least it would mean a dunking, at worst the canoe would be smashed and they'd be out of the race.

She and Brad had scouted it and practiced it until she knew it by heart. First they'd hiked it, and Brad had pointed out the hazards and the line they had to take. Then they'd canoed it several times in the Grumman, the first time stopping at the top to study it once again before shooting through it. Finally, only three days ago, they'd included the stretch in their last training run in the racing canoe.

They worked to get well over to the left. She could hear the river roaring ahead of them. The canoe in front of them went to the right, and Carly thought for a moment they were in deep trouble. They bounced and skidded down the length of a small island, slid past a deadly, sucking four-foot gap between it and the strainerlike roots of a fallen tree, grated along the gnarled, clutching roots, then whirled away down the river, still under a semblance of control.

Then she felt the current grab them and held her breath, her muscles straining as she fought to keep the canoe straight. She was just congratulating herself on how well they were doing when, to her horror, a new hazard loomed. A tree, which certainly hadn't been there when they practiced, was right in the path they had to take, its branches reaching down into the water like the tines of a giant rake.

"Under it," Brad bellowed, ruddering the bow of the canoe to the right. Carly ruddered, then paddled, and then, still paddling, ducked as the trunk threatened to crush her skull. At Brad's thunderous "Hut," she flipped her paddle from left to right and pulled hard as Brad threw in a quick bow rudder to the left.

She had a fleeting glimpse of a small group of spectators and one forlorn team contemplating its broken canoe, and then she and Brad were whizzing off down the river, driving hard toward the left bank to avoid being smashed against the hulking remains of the old railroad trestle. Just ahead of it and to the right, like dragon's teeth, a row of rotting pilings waited hopefully, eager to add another canoe to its tally.

Fear made Carly pull so hard she could feel the shaft of her paddle bend. Praying it wouldn't break, that Brad had built well, she kept at it.

In moments it was over, a harrowing dash through chaos, a crazy blur of disaster barely averted. They shot out beyond the trestle as if propelled out of a cannon, and sailed into calm waters.

"Wahoo!" Brad bellowed in triumph. "Isn't that something?"

Carly was even more excited than he was and splashed him enthusiastically. The first time she'd seen the stretch from the shore, she had been scared spitless. Only her confidence in him had made her brave enough to try it.

Drawing up on the sandbar to the right of the low dam at Oneonta, they scrambled out and portaged the canoe. Now that they were past the worst part, Carly had time to become aware of the weariness that was creeping up on her. The muscles in her shoulders and back felt like Jell-O. But there wasn't the deep, aching exhaustion she'd felt at the end of the race two weeks ago.

"Now comes the hard part," Brad announced as they eased the canoe back into the water.

"Worse than the trestle?" Carly asked fearfully, wondering if he'd purposely not told her about some other awful section.

Brad grinned. "Harder, not worse. Now we find out just how stern the stuff you're made of really is."

Carly grinned back at him with more than a trace of ferocity. "Well, you're in for an education, buster. I'll paddle you into the ground."

Joe was on the scene again behind the Howard Johnson's

restaurant. They got out of the canoe and walked around, working the kinks out of their legs as they wolfed down the cheeseburgers and milk shakes he had brought. Other canoes were constantly coming or going. One team pulled in and sat down at a picnic table complete with tablecloth and silverware and were served barbecued spareribs with all the trimmings by their supporters. Other canoes continued on by, or stopped just long enough to replenish their fluids and snacks.

She'd peeled off her gloves to eat, and Brad reached for her, tenderly took her hands in his. She thought for a moment he was feeling romantic, then realized he wasn't when he turned them, inspecting each one. She was relieved they were only reddened, that no blisters were developing. If he found a blister, he would be pestering her about it for the rest of the race. He kissed her palms fondly, and slightly embarrassed, she glanced over at Joe. He was ostentatiously studying the river. Brad seemed totally unaware of the fact that they were not in private and took her into his arms and kissed her thoroughly.

"You doing okay?" he asked quietly when they came up for air. The depth of concern in his question warmed her more than the kiss had.

"Fine. How about you?" she asked softly, tracing the curve of his lips with the tip of her finger.

"No problem. Shall we be off?"

Once they were under way again, Carly couldn't help wondering what he'd meant about the hard part being yet to come. Then she remembered what he'd said about the second part being mental. He'd warned her that somewhere around Otego she was going to hate him. She'd pooh-poohed that.

"Don't worry, it happens to everybody. I'll be hating you right back," he had answered, and she had heard the grin in his voice.

The first couple of miles after Howard Johnson's, the river was bordered on the right by the flat modern concrete ribbon of Interstate 88. All the bridges were mobbed with spectators. Brad had told her about a hundred thousand people watched or were in the various races during the weekend. Until now, she hadn't believed him.

Below Oneonta, once past the sewage treatment plant, they were in wilderness again, the river meandering through woods and fields, here and there playing tag with the interstate or the tracks of the D & H Railroad. At one point the bank was a steep, eight-foot sandy bluff. Hundreds of holes two inches in diameter were bored into it. Almost every hole had a head in it. The bank swallows either watched them attentively or zoomed in and out, skimming the surface of the water.

There were larger openings in the bank, too. At one, a woodchuck was taking in the sun and spectating leisurely as the canoes paddled past his front porch. Down near the water were the entrances of muskrat burrows.

Another throng greeted them at Otego. Carly heard her name being called and spotted the lanky Millicent Thorpe on the bank, waving. Brad angled them in to the shore.

"Millicent, this is Brad Weston," Carly introduced them hastily. "Where are Greg and Peter?"

"Playing in the mud, what else? Probably ruining the new clothes I bought them with your last check. Nice to see you again," Millicent added to Brad.

"We've met?" he asked, startled.

"Do you need anything?" Millicent asked, apparently not having heard his question.

"Candy bars," Carly answered, digging into her jeans for a couple of damp bills.

"Meet you at the fishing site," Millicent called, heading off to round up her children.

"She seems awful nice to rob," Brad commented as they rejoined the race.

Carly let the comment pass and resumed paddling. "You don't remember her?"

Brad shook his head. "Maybe something with the emergency squad."

"What's the emergency squad?"

"Runs the ambulance for the town," he explained curtly.

"I didn't know you were in that."

"No reason you should. We've never gotten a call while you've been up here."

Carly was surprised. It was a revelation to find Brad was not quite the hermit he pretended to be.

This was the stretch of the river she loved best. It was the section she and Brad had first paddled together. There was the sandbar where he'd given her that unforgettable spanking. The memory gave her a warm feeling down deep inside. She smiled to herself and shivered sensuously. Overhead, "Brad's" horned owl was watching the race, as if contemplating the philosophical implications of mass insanity.

Soon, Brad brought them into the access point where they'd started their first paddle. Millicent was there with a fistful of candy bars and lobbed two to Brad and two to Carly. Greg and Peter were covered with mud from head to toe and were obviously having the time of their lives.

"We'll see you at Unadilla," Millicent called as Brad shoved off.

"Great," Carly yelled, both surprised and pleased, especially since they had somehow missed Joe at Otego.

The race was now a grinding battle with exhaustion and boredom. There was very little current, and Carly had the feeling they were paddling through molasses. Weariness was creeping deep into her, draining the reserves of energy she'd fought to build up with all the training. There were still twenty grueling miles to go. She tried not to think about them, or about the fact that they didn't seem to be moving. She wondered if Brad was really trying. He was supposed to be the strong one, after all. She was about to ask him when she remembered what he'd said about teams always getting into fights about here. If they did, she wasn't going to be the one who started it, she decided determinedly.

Her body went on automatic, leaving her consciousness free to ramble. She found herself thinking of the problems at The Gallery. Business hadn't picked up any, and if the fawn was found, she had no idea where the money to pay for it would come from. The fifty thousand dollars from its sale would no longer be enough, and it was about all The Gallery had left in its account.

"What're you doing back there?" Brad demanded when she became so absorbed in her thoughts that she forgot to paddle.

"Thinking about The Gallery," she answered, guiltily digging in again.

"Judas Priest," Brad growled.

"Sorry," Carly apologized.

"Well just don't burden me with that albatross," he retorted. "I've heard enough about it in the last week."

"I'm sorry," Carly said angrily. "I forgot. You're not interested in my problems."

"Not when you won't listen to any of the advice I've given you."

"God, you Ivy Leaguers disgust me," Carly retorted, her weariness making her bitter. "You're always ready to tell everyone else how to run his life, but you've sure screwed up when it comes to your own."

"Oh, is that what you think?" Brad retorted.

"I don't see you as any kind of a roaring success, hiding away up here in the wilderness. This isn't *Green Mansions*, you know."

"You've heard of the book?" Brad asked, surprised.

"Amazingly enough, you can be literate without a degree from Princeton," Carly shot back.

"Sorry," Brad grunted.

"Did you realize that if we average sixty strokes a minute over ten hours, this damn race will require thirty-six thousand strokes?" Carly asked, trying to change the subject.

"Pretty fancy computation. You just figure it out now, or did you do it ahead with pencil and paper?"

"I just did it. I'm not so dumb as you think I am."

"I never said you were dumb."

"Maybe not. But you sure as hell think it."

"I do not."

"Then stop messing with my head. It's my head, and I'll thank you to keep your overeducated, gold-plated opinions out of it."

"Fine, I will."

"Neanderthal," Carly growled under her breath.

"What was that?"

"I called you a Neanderthal," Carly yelled. God, now her back was starting to ache. Why had she let herself get talked into this?

"A reference to my size and strength, no doubt," he said smugly.

"A reference to your egocentricity . . ."

"Ooooh, big word!"

"And your male chauvinist, Stone Age mentality," she went on.

"If that's the way you feel about me, why the hell are you here?"

"I'm wondering that myself."

They paddled on in grim silence. There were other canoes in sight, ahead and behind, and a similar silence seemed to have fallen over them. The only voices were soft "huts" as sides were switched. Wells Bridge came and went, and Carly barely spared the crowd jamming the bridge a glance.

"Now I remember," Brad announced suddenly.

"Remember what?" Carly was tired of being mad, and any conversation was welcome.

"Where I met Millicent Thorpe."

"Oh?"

"She and her husband were leasing a place up on Flax Island Road," Brad began, talking more to himself than to Carly. "Tractor tipped over on him. I was on the ambulance call. He was dead by the time we got there. Guess he didn't leave her much."

"Not a thing, from what I've seen."

"She seems nice."

"She is."

"Too nice to get swindled by someone like you. Just kidding," he added quickly.

"Now I know why you made this canoe so long," Carly growled.

"Why?"

"So I can't bash your brains out with my paddle and pitch your lifeless body overboard."

The second mention of death sobered her, drove home what she was in danger of losing. She still had a chance to change things. Help me, Great-grandma, Carly pleaded desperately. Help me make him see that I didn't let Pan get sold on purpose.

"You know, you could describe my work as a program for redistributing the nation's wealth," she began hesitantly.

"What?" Brad asked in astonishment.

"Rich collectors pay me for what I have, and I pass the money on to less fortunate people by buying things they no longer want. I transfer money from the rich, who've got too much of it, to the Millicents of the world, who need it."

Brad paddled silently for a few minutes. "You've got a point there," he said at last. "A strange kind of twisted logic, but a good point, nonetheless."

"Besides, by getting so upset about selling what you think are treasures, you're putting a very high value on material goods," Carly pointed out, blessing her great-grandmother for the inspiration. Then, deciding it was now or never, she ventured onto ground that had been taboo between them for weeks, the real cause of the problems between them. "And as for Pan..." she began, and held her breath. She had decided before she came up to Otego that she had to resolve the issue of the fawn, to try to get Brad to understand what had happened. If they didn't iron it out, there would never be real trust between them. As usual, she had put it off to the very last. She waited for Brad to say something.

When he simply continued paddling, acting as if he hadn't heard her, she decided she might as well try again. "He had a *Not For Sale* sign on him."

"Can't your customers read?"

It wasn't exactly the response she was looking for, but it was better than nothing. "That one probably couldn't. He was from Kuwait."

"And the moment he came in the door, you hustled right up to him, smelling money..."

"I wasn't even there! Fred sold Pan while I was up here with you. I'd taken Pan to The Gallery so he'd be safe!"

"Oh." Brad was silent for a moment. "And that's how it happened? You might have told me."

"How? Every time I broached the subject, you said you refused to discuss it."

"I suppose I did. So how much did good old Fred soak the guy for?"

"Fifty thousand."

"Good God!" Brad grunted. "You ready for the dam?"

"I don't think there'd be much market for it," Carly quipped. Was he really beginning to believe her?

"Very funny. Just don't get us in a mess," Brad warned.

"You're the one in the front, you keep us off the rocks."

"You're supposed to be steering."

"Me? Now you tell me!" She wondered whether she was

getting light-headed with fatigue or hope, decided she didn't have time to figure it out now, and studied the approach to Unadilla Dam. At least one canoe had come a cropper there, its broken carcass resting to one side of the eight-foot gap that was the only safe passage through the tumbled boulders and concrete.

Carly paddled hard, ruddered quickly, and the bow of the canoe dipped through the funnellike opening as the current grabbed them. They shot over the four-foot standing wave at the bottom, tipping so far that water slopped in over the gunwhale. Then they were through, racing along with the now swift current.

"Nicely done," Brad complimented her.

"Thanks."

"Have I told you lately that I love you?"

"Not lately," Carly replied, his words warming her and worrying her the way they always did.

"Could have sworn I did last night."

"Oh, was that you?"

"I thought it was. There's Millicent. Looks like she met Joe."

"Hi, Millicent!" Carly called as they sped past the gravel bar. One of Millicent's toddlers tried to pitch a rock into the river and succeeded in almost braining himself when it slipped out of his small hand. Joe Johnson was beside Millicent, and Carly smiled knowingly. What a good match those two would be.

"We'll meet you at the finish line," Millicent called back.

"Ten miles to go. Think you'll make it, squaw?" Brad asked.

"I'll beat you to the finish!"

"That'll be a good trick, considering you're in the stern of the canoe."

Thinking back on the sixty miles of river they had already covered, Carly felt a surge of pride. Her spirits rose and she began to paddle harder. "Come on, Tecumseh, paddle!"

"What do you think this is, a race?" he asked, picking up the pace nonetheless.

"If you really love me, you'll paddle," she answered.

Immediately, he began to paddle faster. "What about you?" he asked.

"What do you mean, what about me?" Carly panted.

"Do you love me?"

"Well," she answered, "I either love you, or I'm crazy as a bedbug for letting you get me into this. Seventy miles is insane."

"Nice of you to give me such a clear choice," Brad responded wryly.

Carly was still wrestling with her feelings. "I think I love you," she said finally.

"My, what a sterling example of courage," Brad retorted in a sneering tone.

"Dammit, Brad . . ."

"Dammit, Brad," he mimicked. "Come on, woman, stick your neck out for a change."

"I stuck my neck out before and look where it got me. Used by a self-centered pseudo-academic imitation of Jackson Pollock and ripped off by an Ivy League Fagin in a three-piece suit."

"Left or right?" Brad was asking her to choose between the two channels ahead. The left was wide and easy, while the right was narrow, twisting, and much more challenging.

"Right," Carly answered curtly.

"I expect an answer when we come out the other end," Brad informed her. Then they were both too busy to talk, and Carly tried to think as she maneuvered the canoe through the twisting channel, past fallen trees and under drooping branches.

What stood out in her mind were memories. Every day was adding memories. This insane race was another in the wild string of memories that being with Brad had built. There was the memory of Orlo's barn, and their first brief paddle on the river. There were memories of Brad's house, his bed, his artistry, his wit. They blended together into a tapestry, a crazy quilt of experiences that left her feeling— something. It was an emotion so powerful, she felt as if she was going to be torn apart by it if she didn't acknowledge it, abandon herself to it.

"Well?" Brad asked as they came out of the narrow channel.

"Shut up," Carly growled. "I'm thinking."

"Well, quit thinking and give me an answer!" Brad ordered.

"Oh, damn," Carly sighed. "I'm too tired to think."

Brad, as if sensing the battle she was waging within herself, was silent. His arms worked like pistons as he drove his paddle into the water. His shirt was stained with sweat above the collar of his life jacket, and Carly felt a crazy urge to touch the back of his neck.

"I love you," Carly said softly, finally caving in to the inevitable.

"What was that?" Brad yelled.

"I love you," Carly repeated loudly. "I love you, you crazy, misbegotten ape! I love you!"

Brad's back straightened.

"But, Brad . . ." His shoulders promptly slumped again.

"What?" he asked warily.

"Do you understand that I didn't mean for Pan to get sold?"

"Yes. I'm sorry I didn't give you a chance to explain sooner. I promise it won't happen again. And I hope you spent the money wisely."

"I didn't spend the money."

"You didn't?"

"Of course I didn't, you lunkhead. As I've explained several times, I've been trying to get Pan back."

"Well, see that you do."

"I've told you, we're trying, but . . ."

"Spend the money," he growled.

"But . . ."

"Redistribute it a little."

"No," Carly said firmly. "Never. But while we're on the subject, what about my profession? Does this mean you've accepted it?"

"Perhaps. But what about mine?" he queried.

"Without people to make canoes, today wouldn't have been possible, would it?"

"Hardly," he said dryly.

"Well then, it's worth it. Why didn't you mention you're a member of the emergency squad?"

"Just never came up. I'm a trustee of the local library, too. Neither of them's any big deal."

"Well, they are to me. Because it means you're not a hermit. It means you are doing your part in the world. Which means I was wrong about you."

Brad grinned. "Well, I'm glad we finally got that settled.

Now, can we please get back to the damn race? Let's show these river rats how real racers do it. Stroke, stroke, stroke, stroke," he chanted, picking up the pace to sixty, then sixty-five strokes a minute.

They swept through Sidney in a rush, and Carly barely glanced at the crowd on the bridge overhead. Energy was flowing into her tired body from a source she'd never suspected of existing. Was it happiness? Emotional delirium? All she knew was, everything was okay, and she and Brad were driving down the river, passing canoes whose occupants drooped with weariness.

Five miles to go, and Carly felt as if she could keep on for the rest of her life.

Three miles to go. Her muscles were beginning to burn with the first signs of oxygen starvation, but she continued to match Brad stroke for stroke. It was as if they were parts of the same machine, tied together by an invisible web, energy flowing from one of them to the other. It was sharing on a level she'd experienced only with him and only on more intimate occasions.

They passed yet another canoe as they rounded a bend, and then there, a half-mile ahead, was the finish line. The bank of the river was jammed with spectators. Brad paddled still harder and faster, and Carly continued to match him, never missing a beat. They passed three more canoes in their class in that last unbelievable dash and glided under the flag-draped finish line.

Working as smoothly as ever, still communicating without words, they coasted over to the dock where willing hands awaited them. Carly let them help her out of the canoe, and then, finally, was able to do what she'd been longing to do for an eternity. She fell into Brad's arms and held on to his lovely, comforting, strong bulk and felt his arms tighten around her.

Finally, sagging with weariness, her arm around Brad's waist, she followed the volunteers carrying the canoe up from the dock to the high bank. When they got to the top, they were each given a small "finisher" trophy.

As they headed toward the barbecue pavilion, Joe Johnson appeared with Peter Thorpe riding on his broad shoulders. Millicent was at his side, Greg in hand.

"Someone's been paging you," he announced, ignoring

the way Peter was tugging at his beard. "They want you in the officials' office."

"Fancy car," Brad observed, surveying the Mercedes 300 D sedan parked outside the office door as they approached.

Inside, Carly stopped dead. "Fred? What are you doing here?" She felt Brad stiffen.

"I've—uh—got something for you," Fred announced after the somewhat awkward introductions. He was plainly offended by their grubby, sweaty state and was trying to be tolerant.

Then he stepped aside. Carly heard a ringing in her ears and would have gone down in a heap if Brad hadn't steadied her.

"I'm all right," Carly assured him in a whisper, reaching out to touch the curve of Pan's neck. He was resting delicately on a cleared spot on the cluttered desk.

"And these," Fred added, shoving a wad of papers at her. "I'm buying you out."

"But . . ." Carly looked at the papers. There was a check on top. For a large amount.

"I found a new partner," Fred explained. "That's his car outside. I assume there won't be any difficulties over this?"

"No," Carly agreed, still dazed and so tired she could hardly think. She couldn't imagine where Fred had gotten the money he'd given her—especially after getting Pan back. It was at least half of what she figured The Gallery was currently worth.

"It seemed our philosophies were just too different," Fred continued when Carly didn't speak. "It's best this way."

"You're right, Fred," said Carly slowly. "No, no problem at all."

Fred smiled briefly, then turned his attention to Brad. "If you ever decide to sell some of your carvings . . ."

"Not likely," Brad said bluntly.

"I suppose not," Fred said awkwardly. "Well, I'd better be going." He was obviously relieved to be escaping.

Carly touched the fawn again and put her free arm around Brad's lovely, strong, sturdy torso. He gave Pan an affectionate pat, and then his arms enfolded her tenderly.

Hours later Brad's arms were around her again. Only this time there was nothing between them—no discord, no clothes, no life vests. His skin felt warm against hers. They smelled of soap from their shared bath, and their trophies and the fawn stood on a table at the foot of the bed, where they could admire them.

"Do you think some day we could win that damn race?" she asked as he stroked her bare back.

"I keep telling you, just finishing it is a victory."

"Like this is?" Carly asked, shifting her hips, feeling the warm, sensuous ecstasy of being loved.

"This isn't a race," he said softly.

"Bet I get there before you," she teased. And then there wasn't any need to talk, and they both concentrated so they could reach this finish line together.

WONDERFUL ROMANCE NEWS!

Do you know about the exciting SECOND CHANCE AT LOVE/TO HAVE AND TO HOLD newsletter? Are you on our *free* mailing list? If reading all about your favorite authors, getting sneak previews of their latest releases, and being filled in on all the latest happenings and events in the romance world sounds good to you, then you'll love our SECOND CHANCE AT LOVE and TO HAVE AND TO HOLD Romance News.

If you'd like to be added to our mailing list, just fill out the coupon below and send it in...and we'll send you your *free* newsletter every three months — hot off the press.

☐ *Yes, I would like to receive your free SECOND CHANCE AT LOVE/TO HAVE AND TO HOLD newsletter.*

Name _____

Address _____

City _____ **State/Zip** _____

Please return this coupon to:

Berkley Publishing
200 Madison Avenue, New York, New York 10016
Att: Irene Majuk

HERE'S WHAT READERS ARE SAYING ABOUT

Second Chance at Love.®

"I think your books are great. I love to read them, as does my family."
—*P. C., Milford, MA**

"Your books are some of the best romances I've read."
—*M. B., Zeeland, MI**

"SECOND CHANCE AT LOVE is my favorite line of romance novels."
—*L. B., Springfield, VA**

"I think SECOND CHANCE AT LOVE books are terrific. I married my 'Second Chance' over 15 years ago. I truly believe love is lovelier the second time around!"
—*P. P., Houston, TX**

"I enjoy your books tremendously."
—*I. S., Bayonne, NJ**

"I love your books and read them all the time. Keep them coming—they're just great."
—*G. L., Brookfield, CT**

"SECOND CHANCE AT LOVE books are definitely the best!"
—*D. P., Wabash, IN**

*Name and address available upon request

Second Chance at Love®

___	07246-X	SEASON OF MARRIAGE #158	Diane Crawford
___	07576-0	EARTHLY SPLENDOR #161	Sharon Francis
___	07580-9	STARRY EYED #165	Maureen Norris
___	07592-2	SPARRING PARTNERS #177	Lauren Fox
___	07593-0	WINTER WILDFIRE #178	Elissa Curry
___	07594-9	AFTER THE RAIN #179	Aimée Duvall
___	07595-7	RECKLESS DESIRE #180	Nicola Andrews
___	07596-5	THE RUSHING TIDE #181	Laura Eaton
___	07597-3	SWEET TRESPASS #182	Diana Mars
___	07598-1	TORRID NIGHTS #183	Beth Brookes
___	07800-X	WINTERGREEN #184	Jeanne Grant
___	07801-8	NO EASY SURRENDER #185	Jan Mathews
___	07802-6	IRRESISTIBLE YOU #186	Claudia Bishop
___	07803-4	SURPRISED BY LOVE #187	Jasmine Craig
___	07804-2	FLIGHTS OF FANCY #188	Linda Barlow
___	07805-0	STARFIRE #189	Lee Williams
___	07806-9	MOONLIGHT RHAPSODY #190	Kay Robbins
___	07807-7	SPELLBOUND #191	Kate Nevins
___	07808-5	LOVE THY NEIGHBOR #192	Frances Davies
___	07809-3	LADY WITH A PAST #193	Elissa Curry
___	07810-7	TOUCHED BY LIGHTNING #194	Helen Carter
___	07811-5	NIGHT FLAME #195	Sarah Crewe
___	07812-3	SOMETIMES A LADY #196	Jocelyn Day
___	07813-1	COUNTRY PLEASURES #197	Lauren Fox
___	07814-X	TOO CLOSE FOR COMFORT #198	Liz Grady
___	07815-8	KISSES INCOGNITO #199	Christa Merlin
___	07816-6	HEAD OVER HEELS #200	Nicola Andrews
___	07817-4	BRIEF ENCHANTMENT #201	Susanna Collins

All of the above titles are $1.95

Prices may be slightly higher in Canada.

Available at your local bookstore or return this form to:

SECOND CHANCE AT LOVE
Book Mailing Service
P.O. Box 690, Rockville Centre, NY 11571

Please send me the titles checked above. I enclose _____ Include 75¢ for postage
and handling if one book is ordered; 25¢ per book for two or more not to exceed
$1.75. California, Illinois, New York and Tennessee residents please add sales tax.

NAME _____

ADDRESS _____

CITY _____ STATE/ZIP _____

(allow six weeks for delivery)   SK-41b